Praise for *American Purgatorio*

"*American Purgatorio* is a triumphant American pica-resque, a thrilling quest poem in the indigenous form of a road novel."　—Benjamin Kunkel, *The Nation*

"A dazzling metaphysical high-wire act—compelling, deeply moving, mordantly funny and disquieting in equal measure, an existential trip that, at times, seems to rearrange the molecules in the air around you as you read it, demanding that you think of the world and your relationship in it in a wholly new way."
　　　　　　　　　　　—*The Sunday Telegraph*

"The ending here took me by surprise. It's what every writer strives for—an event both suprising and in-evitable . . . A serious, admirable novel."
　　　　　　　　—Carolyn See, *The Washington Post*

"Hypnotic . . . It's nearly impossible to summarize in a review without detracting from the impact of the gradually unraveling structure . . . Is this a thriller? Amnesia fiction? A metaphysical road novel? A puzzle? The answer is all of the above, of course."
　　　　　　　　—Joy Press, *The Village Voice*

Jorge Colombo

John Haskell
OUT OF MY SKIN

John Haskell is the author of the novel *American Purgatorio* and of the short-story collection *I Am Not Jackson Pollock*. A contributor to the radio programs *The Next Big Thing* and *Studio 360*, he divides his time between New York and California.

ALSO BY JOHN HASKELL

American Purgatorio

I Am Not Jackson Pollock

OUT OF MY SKIN

OUT OF MY SKIN

John Haskell

FARRAR, STRAUS AND GIROUX

New York

Farrar, Straus and Giroux
18 West 18th Street, New York 10011

Portions of the text have appeared,
in somewhat different form, in
A Public Space, *n+1*, *Vice*, and *Black Clock*.

Library of Congress Cataloging-in-Publication Data
Haskell, John, 1958–
    Out of my skin / John Haskell — 1st ed.
        p.   cm.
    ISBN-13: 978-0-374-29909-5 (alk. paper)
    ISBN-10: 0-374-29909-9 (alk. paper)
    1. Lookalikes—Fiction.   2. Celebrities—Fiction.   3. Los
Angeles (Calif.)—Fiction.   4. Identity (Psychology)—Fiction.
5. Psychological fiction.   I. Title.

PS3608.A79O97 2009
813'.6—dc22

                                                    2008029146

Designed by Jonathan D. Lippincott

www.fsgbooks.com

1   3   5   7   9   10   8   6   4   2

*The author would like to thank Lorin Stein, Athena Kokoronis,
the MacDowell Colony, and especially his sister.*

For Francis Freeman

OUT OF MY SKIN

What happened to me was—not me, but what happened—I'm from New York originally and I moved to Los Angeles to write about movies. Now, instead of writing about movies or people making movies, I was somewhere off the California coast, in the middle of the ocean, writing an article about sharks. A group of scientists had rigged up a fishing boat with winches and scientific instruments, and they'd lowered a stainless-steel cage into the water. They were investigating shark communication, and because I was writing an article about their investigation, I was inside the cage. I was under the water, wearing a wetsuit, and under the wetsuit there were sensors attached to various parts of my body, measuring my heart rate and brain activity, and partly I was thinking about brain activity, but mainly I was thinking about sharks. They'd pretty much guaranteed me a shark attack—something about an anomaly in the ocean current—and so I stood there, or I should say floated there, my back to the boat's hull, holding the steel handrail, listening to the air as it passed from the scuba gear into my lungs. That, plus the pressure of the water, plus the temperature of the water, plus the fact that there was going to be a shark attack, was focusing my attention.

Speckled sunlight was filtering down from the surface of the water and schools of little fish were darting out from the darkness. I noticed pieces of meat floating above the cage. The scientists were chumming for sharks, and the blood from the meat was dissolving in the water. Through the mask on my face I was scanning the water, looking for a shark, knowing the minute I stopped looking, the minute I took my mind off the idea of shark, like a watched pot, that's when a shark would appear. And because I didn't want to miss that appearance, I kept my mind focused on the darkness in front of me, not thinking about anything other than the barely visible darkness. But I must have been thinking something. And I must have been in the middle of thinking it when a white underbelly flashed by, huge and white and slightly above me.

Suddenly the bait was gone. The bait was gone and the shark was gone, but I was still there. And I didn't know what the scientists, looking at the data

from my sensors, were recording, but it was probably
fear. My heart was pounding and my adrenaline was
pumping, and I could feel my fingertips pulsing inside my rubber gloves. I'd seen enough of the shark to
feel its threat, but because I was protected by the
safety of the cage, what would normally seem like
fear, felt to me like the opposite of fear. Not desire
exactly, because I couldn't actually see the shark. But
I was aware of something, just beyond my vision.
And when I say aware, I mean I was sensing, from the
shark, a kind of communication. And since the most
rudimentary form of communication is the expression of desire, I was sensing the shark's desire. And
since one of the things it was desiring was my anni-
hilation, I can't say there wasn't a certain amount of
fear. What I was trying to do was reach out through
that fear, and communicate with this thing. The human brain is capable of receiving millions of neural
signals, and I was trying, from inside the cage, to *send*
signals, to the shark. I wanted to tell the shark that I
understood what it wanted, and that I accepted what
it wanted, and I was just beginning to experience the
freedom of this interspecies conversation when I felt
the cage begin to rise. The scientists were bringing
me up out of the water, and I didn't want to go out.
And I tried to tell them. I tried to signal, through the
sensors attached to my body, that I wasn't ready, that

I was still conducting the experiment. I tried to think those thoughts and send those thoughts, but maybe the sensors weren't working, or maybe my thoughts weren't working. Either way, I felt the weight of the water pushing me down as the cage rose up, like an elevator, and there I was again, in the breathable normality of air.

The cage was set down on its special platform, and when the door was opened I remember ducking through the opening and stumbling out onto the relative stability of the deck. Although I was standing on the deck, I was still experiencing what had happened a few moments earlier. I felt almost weightless, like air, only lighter than air, my head like a balloon floating on the top of my spine. I could feel my lungs expanding, and I could hear voices talking and metal clinking against metal. People were standing in front of me, and as I stepped out of the cage I embraced, first the captain, who extended a hand, and then an assistant scientist, who brought me a mug of tea. More than embrace her, I locked my arms around her waterproof jacket. She wore overalls and rubber boots, and I could hear her asking if I was all right. I don't remember what I said exactly, but I must have been grinning, and it must've been an infectious grin, because when she led me to a plastic crate, she was grinning at me.

I sat there, still in the wetsuit, the electronic

wafers still taped to my body, a blue blanket around my neck, my butt bones on the plastic crate, my feet on the deck, the ocean in front of me, the sky above me, and the only thing missing was my thought. I noticed a corroded hinge on the cabin door, and instead of thinking about what kind of paint they used to paint the hinge, or imagining how I would paint the hinge if I owned the boat, instead of reacting to the hinge, I just saw what it was. Every so often I noticed a thought slip into my head, but it was easy enough to let it go and return my attention to the hinge. Or the assistant scientist. Her long hair was falling across her wide blue eyes. She was standing in front of a portable control panel, asking me questions, measuring my physiological responses, telling me that although she hadn't done it yet, she wanted to go under the water herself. She told me her name was Elena, that she was an intern, and we talked about Dramamine and UCLA and the life of a marine biologist. There I was, holding my mug of warm tea, looking at her face and the peaceful horizon behind her face, and I wouldn't have called it paradise exactly, but if paradise is a place where the need for protection falls away, then that's where I was.

And the only question is: How long does it last?

I was drinking my tea, tasting the tea and the sugar in the tea, and seeing this person in front of me, her teeth when she smiled, and the gums above her teeth. And her lips. The shape of her lips reminded me of a certain movie star, and I began thinking about the various roles I'd seen that particular movie star play, and while I was thinking, and while I was involved in the various narratives that led from that thinking, I wasn't actually seeing the wide blue eyes of the assistant scientist. It wasn't that I wasn't paying attention; I didn't even know I wasn't paying attention. I was sitting there, in the middle of what might have been a normal conversation, and I was creating, not a cage exactly, but a sense of who I was.

I'd been living with a woman in New York. When she moved out of the apartment we shared, I lived there a while longer, but the magazines I'd been writing for didn't pay enough to support living there alone. And I didn't want to live there alone. And since I'd been thinking about moving to Los Angeles, that's what I did. I put most of what I owned in storage, and the second thing I did when I arrived was buy a car, an old Toyota Camry. I was giving myself a month to test the waters of California, and since I wasn't sure what I would be doing, instead of renting an apartment, the first thing I did was find a downtown hotel offering rooms by the month—the Hotel Metropole—and that's where I was living.

Alan, the one who told me I should "come to L.A. and write about movies," worked for the *Los Angeles Times*, and at the moment I was sitting with him, at a low table in a nostalgic bar off Wilshire Boulevard, talking about a piece he wanted about celebrity impersonators. I don't know why Alan chose that particular bar, but I call it "nostalgic" because, whether or not it actually existed in the 1950s, it was made to seem as if, sitting at the low table, with the bamboo walls and the Polynesian masks, you were somewhere in the middle part of the last century. It was a cultural memento, or more accurately, a memento mori; the past it referred to, the playboy, beach-party aesthetic that came into being after World War II, had long since passed away. The photographs on the walls— publicity stills of movie stars like Dean Martin and Tony Curtis—were cultural souvenirs, bits of the past, and like the past, they were mutable. Because I'd been thinking about changing my own name I was aware, for instance, that Dean Martin was born Dino Crocetti, that Tony Curtis was Bernard Schwartz, and that

Barbara Stanwyck, in her flowing gown, was originally Ruby Stevens.

Anyway, I was sitting there with Alan, and next to Alan was a tall young woman named Jane, an ex-dancer apparently, who wanted to learn about photography. She had a short, boyish haircut, and although she wasn't all that garrulous, the conversation seemed to flow. Alan, who was trying to get me work at the *Times*, did most of the talking. I'd come to Los Angeles knowing only two people, and one of them was Alan, and this woman was an acquaintance of his, someone he wanted to be an acquaintance of mine, a romantic acquaintance. And although I also wanted that, I was still slightly uncomfortable jumping into the ocean of romance. That's what it seemed like, an ocean, and Alan's way of pushing me into the water of that ocean was to introduce me to this person.

We were drinking our drinks and talking about photography, and I said to her, "Alan told me you wanted to know about cameras."

"I think I have the camera part figured out," she said, and she reached into her bag and pulled out a film camera with adjustable dials and levers.

Alan, a mojito in one hand, a cheese cracker in the other, sat back in his chair, so that the triangle formed by the three of us left him slightly removed. He'd told her I knew something about photography—

which wasn't an absolute lie, because I did take pictures—but I certainly wasn't an expert, and I told Jane, "I really don't know that much."

"Don't let him fool you," Alan said. "He's got an outstanding eye."

"That's what I want to develop," she said.

"Then he's your man."

Alan had the habit of treating people as if they were stupid, not because he believed they were, but because by assuming they were, until they told him otherwise, he was able to feel safe.

My way to feel safe was different. A writer in Los Angeles is fairly far from the top of the food chain, and I wanted to seem a little more substantial, a little more sure of myself than I actually was. I sat with my back straight, my collarbones extended, and I looked into her eyes in what I hoped was a meaningful way. I told her about the two books I'd written, and she told me she also wrote books, young-adult novels. We started talking about books and photography, and I noticed, when she smiled, that her teeth, although they were white, were not quite even, and as I looked at them I tried to imagine what it would be like to love uneven teeth, and by extension, the person behind the teeth.

Unless Alan had hired a prostitute. There was always the possibility that this was a joke he was playing, on me. He'd mentioned something about a life she'd had before the life she was living now, but I didn't care, and she didn't seem to care, and we talked like that for a while, but the talking isn't what I'm getting at. The talking was pleasant, but it was preparatory. What really happened, happened later, when we took Alan up on his suggestion and walked outside.

He'd suggested we stop talking about photographs and actually do it. So we finished our drinks, stood up, and "You two go," he said. "I have to take this call."

I don't know if there actually was a call, but we left Alan, walked through the lunchtime drinkers, past the bamboo walls of photographs, and when we opened the heavy wooden doors, suddenly there was light. It took a while for our eyes to adjust to the light, and when they had, I asked her where she wanted me to stand. She was going to take my picture.

"Where do you think?" she said.

We were standing at the edge of the parking lot. The cars were in bright sunlight, and from what I knew about photography I knew it required light, so I suggested I stand in the sun. "I'll stand by this car," I said, staking out an area next to an expensive-looking black sedan.

She told me, at one point, to do something.

"Do what?"

"You're the model," she said. "Right? Everyone thinks it's so easy."

I didn't know how I wanted to stand, or how she wanted me to stand, and "How much are you taking?" I said, meaning how much of my body was caught by the frame of the camera.

"Act like you're walking."

I tried to do that.

"I mean, really walk."

And I walked, but apparently I walked too fast, or too slow. And it would be safe to say that things, literally, weren't clicking. I made an attempt to strike a pose, and she didn't say anything, but I could tell that she didn't like it, and I said, "If you were me, getting your photograph taken, how would you stand? Here," I said, and took out my little silver camera and pointed it at her.

She was standing next to a car, in her sleeveless dress, still holding her camera. She gave me a look and she said, "I'd stand like this."

I took the picture.

And because that seemed to relax her, I took another, and then when she seemed to get more comfortable, I said, "Now me," and I stood in the same way she'd stood, and she was looking through the camera at me, and I could hear that she wasn't taking the picture. "Go ahead," I said. "Take it." Although I was the one in front of the camera, she was the one who was nervous. And I told her, "It doesn't have to be perfect," but she said she wasn't sure about the light. "Don't worry about light. Work with me, baby," I said, and did a fake fashion-model imitation.

I was joking, but she was serious, telling me about the difficulty she was having with the light and the focus, and while she was talking I lifted my camera and took another picture—of her. And when I did, she stopped concentrating on her camera and started concentrating on me.

I thought she might like to use my camera, and I held it out to her. "I think it adjusts automatically for the light," I said, but instead of responding, she just stood there. So I took another picture. I didn't know what I was doing, but because she seemed to assume I did, I took another, and then another. I moved so that the sun was off to the side, and she put her camera on the hood of a car, moved away from the car, and away from her camera, and she began moving her hands, not to any purpose, except the purpose of looking good. That was her default mode, a mask she was comfortable in, and I was behind my own mask, snapping the pictures.

And sometimes you need a mask. Like the steel bars of a shark cage, sometimes you need to feel safe enough to express something that exists behind the mask. And that's fine, except in our case, instead of

14

allowing us, from a place of safety, to reveal who we were, the masks did what masks are supposed to do, they hid who we were.

I suggested we "take one of each other, at the same time." But she didn't seem to be listening anymore. She was lost now in what she was doing, in the role she had taken, the role of a model, and now she was in it, and as I kept shooting photographs of her, photograph after photograph, I could feel our relationship carving its rut. And it wasn't a bad thing, this rut, it was still very shallow, but it was getting deeper and deeper, and because it was a rut, we continued to communicate in this way. She was letting me know what she wanted, and she was sensing what I wanted, and I wasn't telling her where to stand or how to stand, she was just standing there, posing, and I let her pose, and I continued taking photographs.

I'd gone to see a play, a revival of Bertolt Brecht's *Life of Galileo*. The shark story had been rejected, and now I was doing a piece about a man named Scott, who was in the play—he played Galileo—and what made him different than any other struggling actor in Los Angeles was that he was a celebrity look-alike. His job was to look like Steve Martin. Steve Martin was a popular movie star at the time, and although in the play it didn't quite work, in his life Scott supported himself by pretending to be the charming, and famously white-haired, movie comedian.

I'd gone to what he called his house in Laurel Canyon. It was actually a garage, a barely converted garage situated slightly below a large house, tucked into the eucalyptus hillside. His living area was a narrow room partitioned off from the rest of the garage, with a narrow bed, a table beside the bed, a brown rug, and a fake-wood dresser. A miniature television was on top of the dresser, playing an old movie, *Detour*. I knew the movie because a pivotal character in the story was a man named Haskell.

"I leave it on all day," he said, referring to the television, and then he led me through a doorway-sized hole cut into the drywall, into another area, with a sink and a toilet and a shower that drained into the garage floor. The only thing recommending the place was a deck he had outside. If you walked around the garage to this redwood deck, you were suddenly looking over a wild and natural canyon. Across the canyon you could see the backs of a few houses through the trees.

I was standing with him on the deck, and he was telling me that, although he slept in the garage, he also had what he called "Steve's office" in a room in the old Bank of America building, on the corner of Hollywood and Ivar. That's where he kept his Steve Martin gear. We were talking specifically about gear, and generally about the life of a celebrity look-alike.

"It's a state of mind," he told me.

This was probably true because, although he was thin, and had the white hair and the easy smile, he bore only a passing resemblance to the celebrity actor he was paid to imitate.

"It really doesn't matter what I look like," he said. "It's the white hair. It's a trick."

We were standing near some steps that led off the deck and into the canyon, and I think because we shared a body type, not even Steve Martin's body type exactly, but because we had a similar posture, he was telling me about his life, that he'd come to Los Angeles to act, and although he enjoyed the Steve Martin routine, he was tired of playing the same part every day. He said he wanted to get away.

"From L.A.?"

"Everything."

I brought out my recording device, thinking I would start recording our conversation, but his idea for the interview was to take a walk. I followed him down the steps of the deck, past a grapevine with grapes ripening on the branches. He pulled one off and handed it to me.

"No thanks," I said.

"Right off the vine?"

I took the small round grape and thanked him, but instead of eating the grape, I put it in my jacket pocket. Then he led me down a narrow trail, and it didn't take long before we found ourselves at the bottom of the canyon, standing in front of an opening to a runoff drain. There was a trickling rivulet of water, and I didn't know the difference between a runoff drain and a sewer tunnel, but whatever it was he assured me it was safe to walk through.

"What's in there?" I said.

"The tunnel."

"I mean what's in the tunnel," I said, but apparently the tunnel was more than simply a route to get somewhere, because he bent down, and straddling the rivulet, he started walking into the tunnel, his feet braced against the sloping concrete sides. I could see past him to a faint pinpoint of light at the other end of the tunnel, and as he got deeper into the tunnel, all I could see was his outline. He was calling to me, "Are you coming?"

"I don't think so."

"Come on."

"I don't . . ." My words were echoing off the walls of the tunnel.

It wasn't just water he was walking through.

There was mud and debris, and occasionally I would hear him step in something, or on something, and although I could hardly see him, or maybe *because* I could hardly see him, he reminded me of Charlie Chaplin. He was walking along, his feet splayed out like the Little Tramp, and I saw in his posture an optimism, the optimism of Los Angeles. People come here to escape an old life, or to exchange an old life for something else, or better, and although the old life tends to follow you, there's always optimism. In the movies, Los Angeles is usually portrayed as a paradise, and because paradise is a place of possibility, I was thinking I should just walk inside the tunnel, and I was about to do it when Scott emerged from the tunnel's opening. He stood in the weeds, blinking his eyes, adjusting to the light.

"So." He turned to me. "That was the tunnel."

As far as I could tell, this had nothing to do with his impersonation of Steve Martin, and so, when we climbed up the canyon and back onto his deck, I thought we'd be starting our interview. There weren't any chairs on the deck so we both stood. The light was filtered by the trees. "I should probably ask you a few questions," I said, "about Steve Martin."

"Plenty of time for that," and he climbed up onto the redwood railing that enclosed the deck. He reached up and there was a rope, one end looped around a nail and the other end tied to a tree branch overhanging the canyon. He took the rope, pulled it off the nail, and said, "It's a swing. You want to go?"

"I'm fine," I said. I mentioned my bad ankle.

"It's not dangerous," he said. "It's fun," and with one foot on the redwood railing, he slipped his other foot into a loop at the end of the rope, his hands gripping a knot in the rope. "It's totally safe," he said, and then he kind of hopped into the air, cleared the railing, and swung out over the canyon. He yelled something, mid-swing, and then he swung back, landed on the railing, and steadied himself by holding on to the roof of the house. "This will blow your mind," he said, and he stepped down off the railing and held the rope out to me.

I didn't take the rope, not at first. And it's possible I didn't take it because of an old ankle injury, but it's also, probably more possible, that I was comfortable where I was and being what I was, and although I didn't necessarily like what I was, I didn't want to have to be scared.

But Scott's enthusiasm was infectious. Since it looked like a high-tech mountain-climbing rope, and since I was ostensibly engaged in participatory journalism, and since I wanted to get an idea of what his life was like, what it was like to be a Steve Martin look-alike, I took the rope. "I'm not going to jump,"

I said. "I just want to get a sense, of . . ." And he helped me up onto the railing.

As a launching pad it was slightly too narrow. I was having trouble balancing, so Scott held the shin of my left leg. "Put your foot in the loop," he said, "as a safety precaution. In case you fall." And I wanted to be safe, so I centered the ball of my right shoe into the rope's loop. I was standing there, holding the rope, one foot on the two-by-four rail and one foot slightly raised, and because the side of the canyon was steep, I could see that if I swung I'd be swinging out several stories above the canyonside. I don't know how many feet it was, but quite a few, and I pictured the rope breaking and me falling, and I turned to Scott, ready to abort the whole project, and that's when he let go of my shin.

I thought I'd been standing on my own, balancing myself just fine, but when he released me, at first I wobbled a bit, and then, because of the weight of the rope, or my own weight, whatever it was, I started to tilt. I started to go, and once I started, I went. I swung out over the edge of the railing, down and out and over the canyon, which fell away below me. And I have to say it was great. The thrill, first of all, that was great, and the view was amazing, and the weightlessness. For a moment, at the top of the arc of my swing, I was absolutely weightless. The trees were below me and the emptiness was below me, and I was floating above them, untethered from everything I knew. And at the same time I was part of everything, and I could see every detail clearly. And the thing was, I seemed to stay up there, taking it all in, longer than normal. And then I swung back.

I swung down into the canyon and up toward the deck, but unlike Scott I didn't manage to land on the railing, so I swung out again, and this time the view wasn't as good. I was thinking about the deck, which seemed to be far away, and thinking about the sound of the rope rubbing against the tree, and when I swung back again Scott tried to grab my hand, but because of the way the rope was fastened to the tree, I started twirling around. I started rotating, like the earth rotating on its axis, swinging out over the canyon, catching glimpses of the deck as I rotated, then swinging back to the deck, back and forth like that, until Scott finally reached out to me with the handle of a broom. I was able to grab the end of the handle, and he pulled me back to the relative stability of the deck. It took a few seconds before the swinging in my head gradually subsided, until the rotating slowed and the spinning faded away, and then Scott looked at me.

"Do you feel it?"

I knew what he was talking about. "Yes," I said, referring to the sense of freedom, and I looked at him, and I started remembering the feeling I'd had a few moments earlier.

"For a second there," he said, "you almost had it."

I'd seen the *Life of Galileo* in a theater not that far from the theater where the play was originally performed in 1947. Ingrid Bergman and Charlie Chaplin and Billy Wilder—along with Brecht, who wrote the play—were all there on opening night, and although reviews at the time were mixed, the play is now part of theater history. Charles Laughton, who worked with Brecht on the translation, played the role of Galileo, and what happened to the famous scientist was, in a way, happening to me.

Galileo had discovered a new way of thinking about the world (that the earth revolved around the sun). However, by proving it, he was seen as undermining the dominant authority (in his case the Catholic church). And that was a problem. In the beginning it wasn't a huge problem because the pressure on him was to voluntarily change his mind. But Galileo was adamant in his belief, and vocal, and because he was unwilling to disbelieve the facts in front of his eyes, he was put on trial. An inquisition found him guilty of heresy and he was asked to recant. I say "asked," but the choices they gave him were somewhat limited. Did he want to change his beliefs or did he want to be tortured? It was 1633, and torture hasn't changed that much, and although he was certainly a great scientist and possibly a great man, he needed a little protection, and the only way he knew to get that protection was to renounce what he knew to be true.

In the play, Galileo is assisted by a young man named Andrea, a prize student who not only assists, but worships Galileo, in the way a son worships a father. When the authorities take Galileo away, Andrea is sure his mentor won't submit. He's young and idealistic, and he believes in the power of protest. He believes a person, if necessary, should die for a cause. The play makes it clear that although Galileo practices the austerity of a life of science, he also enjoys his comfort, and in one scene near the end of the play, Andrea visits Galileo in his comfortable cell. At this point, because Galileo has already recanted, Andrea is feeling betrayed. When he confronts his teacher, Galileo just stands there, hands in his pockets, unconcerned or unaware of what seems to Andrea like an unforgivable moral collapse.

"Why did you recant?"

"They showed me the instruments of torture," Galileo says. For him, it's not about idealism. It's about pain. "I don't like pain."

And like any son, Andrea wants him to protest. He wants his hero to rage against blindness and dogma, and when he sees that there is no rage, that there's only resignation in the watery eyes, he takes the love he feels and he tries to extinguish it. And that's when Galileo gives Andrea the book. He's been writing his theories in a secret book, called the *Discorsi*, and he gives the book to Andrea, who smuggles it out of Italy, and with it, alters the course of history.

 When I left New York, I left not only the life I'd had, but the social entanglements, and although I didn't want to replicate those entanglements in Los Angeles, I did want some human contact. So I called Jane, the ex-dancer. I wanted to get to know her better, and as a way to do that, I told her I was writing an article about her neighborhood. I asked if she would want to help, and

she said she would, so the next day I drove to her house for an interview. The story was supposed to be about the changing demographic in Echo Park, where she lived, in a stucco house with a big black dog named Rex. She answered the door wearing sweat pants and a faded red T-shirt, and we shook hands. She set me up in her so-called recreation room, on a beanbag chair, looking out to the lemon trees in her backyard. We talked about photography and her camera, and she told me she wasn't actually interested in cameras, that she'd just been pretending, and that if she wanted a photograph she used the camera in her phone.

While I was setting up the microphone she made two cups of tea. She brought them into the room on a wooden tray, and because the beanbag chair was in the corner of the room, she had to reach over me to set the tea on the table. Partly it was the lavender scent she was wearing, and partly it was the fact that I'd just seen the movie *Notorious*, with Cary Grant and Ingrid Bergman. In the lobby of my hotel they'd set up a television that played old movies, and it wasn't that I was comparing her with Ingrid Bergman, but when she sat down, cross-legged on a pillow, I noticed a kind of Ingrid Bergman beauty in her cheekbones. In the movie, Ingrid Bergman played a kind of prostitute, and I was going to ask Jane about

her experience with prostitution in the neighborhood when she started explaining to me about the
young-adult fiction she was writing. She said it was
aspirational, meaning that her readers were aspiring
to be different. She was sitting on the pillow, with the
microphone on the beanbag naugahyde between us,
and as she talked I was looking at her face, which was
thoughtful yet playful, and I felt attraction. Her looks
and her manner were easy and natural, and I liked
her. And it's natural, when you like someone, to want
the feeling reciprocated. And to facilitate that recip-
rocation, I sat up in the beanbag, pressing my shoulder blades deeper into my back, hoping a change in
my posture would effect a reaction in her. But she
didn't seem to notice. She was concentrating on the
microphone, trying to be interesting and articulate
for the readers of the magazine I was supposedly writing for.

"Their personalities," she said, "are like the bones
of babies," and when she gestured, she looked at me,
and she asked me, "Do you have any children?" I told
her I didn't, and she nodded—she paused first, then
nodded—and as I watched her talking I was thinking
that yes, she was an author now, but she hadn't always
been an author. I thought I was seeing through the
role of author, through her interest and expressive-
ness, to who she really was. I thought I was being

perceptive until I realized there was something about the way she was sitting on her pillow, with the sunlight hitting the side of her face, her hands waving in the air, and the fact that she was honestly answering my questions. Although I thought I was seeing her role, in actual fact, she wasn't playing any role.

And it's easy to say to someone, Be yourself, and I could have said it to her, but because she *was* being herself, I began thinking about who I was. I was feeling a tightness in my chest, which is usually an indication that I'm about to do something or say something to spoil an otherwise enjoyable experience. And what I did, in response to that, was think of someone who would do something different. I thought about Steve Martin, but I didn't know many Steve Martin movies, and since I'd just seen a Cary Grant movie, and because Cary Grant, in the history of leading men, was someone I didn't mind emulating, I tried to act like him. I didn't talk like Cary Grant or do a Cary Grant imitation, but I tried to relax. And in that relaxation I became a little more honest. I told her what I was doing. I admitted that I wasn't really writing a magazine story about her neighborhood. And that's when Jane suggested we take a walk.

"You can leave the microphone," she said, and she put Rex on a leash and we set off, up through the eucalyptus trees behind her house. She lived near

Elysian Park, and we were walking Rex up the trails, traversing the hillside, and Rex, old as he was, seemed to love to be outside, smelling the world. He was running ahead, off his leash now, happy to be sniffing the various stumps and bushes and clumps of leaves. She told me the main reason she chose the house was so Rex could have the park. "Rex is quite a dog," I said, and she said that he was indeed quite a dog.

"He's old," she said, "but he's photogenic," and she brought out her phone and showed me what seemed to be a collection of photos. There was Rex with his paw in the air, and Rex eating his food, and Rex sleeping, and then there was a photo of what appeared to be a naked woman's body, in a bathtub. And then she closed her phone.

"Who was that?" I said. "That wasn't Rex."

"I don't know how that got on there."

She turned toward Rex so that I couldn't see her face, but I assumed the photo was a photo of her, and as I watched her running after Rex, in my mind I began combining the two images, her in her sweat pants and T-shirt, and the naked body lying in the tub.

Cary Grant was born Archibald Leach, in England. He left school early, joined a troupe of acrobats, began acting, and then he changed his name. It was to a young Cary Grant that Mae West said her famous line, "Why don't you come up sometime and see me?" In those first films, although he'd taken the name of Cary Grant, he was still developing a character different than the character of Archibald Leach. With time, however, the Cary Grant he named himself became the Cary Grant he was, and I wanted to be like that. Not changing my name, but changing what I was. I wanted to be what he was, and since partly what he was was an acrobat, I started climbing onto the rocks. There were some large boulders next to the trail and I started walking on those. Rex, who was panting at this point, stayed on the trail watching me, and Jane was also watching, and I was glad she was watching.

"You're being careful, I hope."

I was standing on a steep part of a round boulder. I told her my shoes were very sticky.

"It looks precarious."

And I wanted it to look precarious. She was athletic, and I seemed to be impressing her with my athleticism. So I continued doing what seemed to be working. I ran ahead, feeling good, not quite like Cary Grant, but acrobatic like him, and jumping like him, and in the physical activity of hopping from rock to rock, whatever thoughts I had, about who I was other than Cary Grant, disappeared.

Apparently, in the field of memory acquisition, one school of research claims that very young children actually have no memory, that because their experience of the world is so new, when they see a tree, they can't compare it with other trees because they haven't seen enough trees to make the comparison. What would normally be processed as memory gets sent to a part of the brain in charge of pure experience. And it was pure experience for me, scampering along the rock ledge, running along, watching the rock where my foot would land, and then, before it landed, looking for the next rock, trusting my foot to land on the rock I'd seen a half second earlier.

I wasn't being a complete Cary Grant, but because I was letting Cary Grant take over the jumping, it got to the point where I felt light, like air, and as I glided over the rocks, part of me was thinking about weightlessness and part of me was thinking about the end of *Notorious*. That's when Cary Grant, who until that time had been judgmental and disdainful toward Ingrid Bergman, was able to see her, not as a spy or a slut or an alcoholic brat, but as a woman whose love he could possibly return.

And that's when I fell.

I thought I was pretty good at telling which rocks were stable, and I thought this particular jump was an easy jump. But the rock I was jumping on, which had seemed solid and stable, moved, and my ankle, which was already weak, twisted. And when I fell I could tell I was hurt, not seriously, but enough to know I should probably put some ice on it. Or at least go back to my hotel.

Which I did.

I said goodbye, limped back to my car, and drove to the Metropole. The tenants were gathered in the lobby, sitting on sofas and chairs around the television set, and I got my keys from Earl, the man at the desk. He was reading an old paperback book by Raymond Chandler, and we talked, briefly, about Raymond Chandler and drinking oneself to death, and then I walked up to my room on the third floor. It had a bed and a dresser and a chicken-wire ceiling stretched across the yellow partition walls. I'd bought the script of Brecht's *Life of Galileo*, and I lay back on the thin mattress, my foot elevated on the metal bedstead, my head on a folded pillow, and I was holding the book, but instead of reading the book, I was thinking about Jane.

In the course of my life I'd fallen in love a number of times. Falling in love with a person was one thing, the flirtation and attraction were all familiar to me, but *being* in love with a person, that was something I hadn't had much luck with. Which was why I'd come to Los Angeles. Which was why I was intrigued by Scott. Which was why, the next day, he picked me up in front of the Metropole and took me to the place where he was going to change who he was.

I was sitting in the passenger seat of his blue Honda hatchback, the floorboard filled with papers and metallic wrappers, driving with him to a job he had, a birthday party in Eagle Rock. He was dressed up in a Steve Martin suit, telling me about a certain song he'd been hearing in his head that answered a question I'd asked about his theory of being Steve. That's what he called it. He told me the crucial part of what he did was noticing, not just his thoughts, but the attitude behind those thoughts.

He was saying things I knew I would never remember, so I pulled out my recorder.

"You have thoughts, right?" he said. "But do you notice them?"

I was fiddling with my earplug headphones, trying to get the volume right.

"I do," he said. "If I'm going to be Steve Martin, I better know which thoughts are his and which are mine. Or else people will know I'm faking."

I looked up. "You *are* faking."

"Good point," he said, and he reached over and took a digital music player from the glove compartment. He was steering the car with one hand, and with his other hand he was holding his music player, searching his song collection, trying to find a certain song as a way to explain what it was to be another person.

"It's not thought," he said. "It's *pre* thought." He was telling me this, gesturing to me as a way of explaining, but because he was driving the car, his gestures were abbreviated. And when he said, "We all have attitudes," I said, "By 'we' you mean . . ."

"Everybody." He made a gesture of possibility. "Every second a million thoughts are zipping through our brains; we either like them, or we hate them, whatever. We don't notice how they're creating us."

I told him I thought I knew what he was talking about, and I would have been a little more attentive, except now he was asking me to steer the car.

"Take the wheel."

So I put my hand on the steering wheel, and while I was steering the car, he was searching for this one particular song he wanted, a Bob Marley version of a certain Beatles song. He had one earplug in his ear and he was holding the other one to me, which I put in my ear, and when he found the song, he played it, and this led to another song he had to play for me, a Jefferson Airplane song from the sixties, which led to a Joni Mitchell song, which reminded me of Jane. Not that Jane looked like Joni Mitchell, but in my mind I was making the connection. And then he found— and played for me—a particular recording of a certain Burmese monk.

Although we were on the freeway, and the steering was fairly straightforward, I was having a little trouble doing several things at once. I was listening to him in one ear, listening to his music in the other ear, trying to record what he was saying, and also steering the car. Not only that, but because he had his foot on the gas pedal, I was having to tell him to slow down or speed up, and since he was the one who knew where we were going, even though he was scanning the songs in his collection, he was giving me directions. So I was glad when he took back the wheel and pulled onto an off-ramp that led to the area of town we were going.

The house was at the top of a hill, and we parked down from the house and walked together—he as Steve Martin, me as me—past a security guard, through a gate, and into an expansive yard. Scott had his special arrow in his hand, the one he would put on his head that would seem to go *through* his head, "the crowd pleaser," he called it. He was wearing a flower, from a neighbor's wildflower garden, in his lapel.

About twenty-five kids were scattered around the backyard pool area, and the minute they saw him they dropped their inflatable toys and guns and ran to him. Obviously they'd been told a clown was coming, but when they got close enough to see that he wasn't actually a clown, not the kind of clown they were counting on, I could see the disappointment in their unwrinkled faces.

There were girls and boys, racially and ethnically mixed, and I noticed they weren't all overweight. It was a birthday party for one of them, one of the Mexican kids, who was eight. They were all about eight, and they took one look at Scott, who was looking like Steve Martin, and they didn't understand. They knew what a clown was, and this man, who was supposed to be a clown, looked like the parents they were hoping to escape from. They knew enough to know that clowns had big noses and baggy pants, and although I'm sure Scott could sense the disappointment, he persisted. This was his job, and so he started in doing a few funny bits, walking funny and talking funny. "Early Steve Martin," he called it. I would almost have called it "desperate Steve Martin" because his interpretation of Steve Martin was unrecognized except by the adults. They were all standing near the house, holding drinks, either smiling or laughing, but the kids were just watching. They hadn't run away, but it was clear he had a tough crowd.

And that's when Scott squatted down and spoke to the kids, face to face. I was getting my microphone ready, so I didn't see when he fell on the ground—a pratfall, I suppose—and I didn't hear exactly what he was saying, but some of the kids started giggling and touching each other on the head, and touching Scott's head, becoming comfortable with this new thing that was neither adult nor child. And not quite a clown. What he was doing was being something they didn't have. He was an adult who was also one of them. Not exactly one of them, but something like a friend. Their rich parents were clearly not friends, but this funny man with the white hair was silly, and silly was the same as vulnerable, and vulnerable was what they felt most of the time, living in an adult world they knew almost nothing about.

People who have the gift of letting go of themselves enjoy the gift because, by letting go of who they are, they can afford to let go of what doesn't work. And the trick, it seemed to me, is to have something waiting, another self or another way of being, something, so that in the moment of letting go, in the sensation of that sense of nothingness, there's something to hold on to.

I walked past the pool filled with brightly colored

flotation devices, and I stood by the house, near a sliding glass door, with the other adults. I stood, watching Scott, and watching my expectations of what was possible dissolve. It wasn't about weightlessness; it was very down-to-earth. The Steve Martin shtick was integrated, not only into his actions but into his attitude, and I could see that in being with the kids he was completely connected to them. In spite of their initial skepticism, and the implicit ridicule of that, he persevered, and where before the Steve Martin look-alike mask had seemed pathetic to me, now it seemed like a pretty good alternative, and instead of judging him, now I wanted, at least momentarily, to be him.

Alison was the other friend I had living in Los Angeles. She'd left New York about four years earlier and now, as a way to introduce me to Angelino culture, she'd invited me to a bookstore, for the launching of a new magazine. Its aim, according to the press release, was the "fusion of fashion and literature," and along with the wine, there were various people reading from texts. By the middle of the second reader, a poetess, Alison informed me, not quite sotto voce, that she was leaving. She probably wanted me to leave with her, but because the event was part of my new life in Los Angeles, I decided to stay.

And I did.

And while I was standing there, listening to a man reading an essay about the Woodstock music festival, I noticed the neck of a woman in front of me. The bookstore hadn't bothered with chairs so most of us were standing, and while the man was reading his excerpt about the use of drugs—not only at Woodstock, but in what he called the general culture of rebellion—saying that drugs were a protest against the old, a tool to get closer to reality, I was focused on this neck, and the downy hairs on the back of the neck. This was a neck I knew, and when the man finished, and after we clapped, the woman turned around.

I was about to say something to her but she spoke first.

"I know you."

"Sure," I said. "How's Rex?"

"He's great."

I was good with the names of animals.

"How's your ankle?"

"Fine," I said, and I didn't know what to say and she didn't seem to mind.

She was wearing glasses now, and a beret on her head, and a yellow dress with straps. She started telling me about some award she was a finalist for, and that she enjoyed our "quote interview," and that's when a woman walked up, kissed her on both cheeks, and then a man walked up and said, "Tell Jane about Mammoth," and for a while they talked about their vacation.

And when the couple left we stood there, and it was like meeting her for the first time. I wanted to tell her she looked like Joni Mitchell.

"With that beret . . ." I said.

"It's French."

"Of course," I said, and there was a pause.

I knew that Joni Mitchell, during the time of the Woodstock music festival, had a chance to go there and play her music. She was invited to take a plane with some musicians she knew, with Crosby and Stills and Nash, but she'd also been scheduled to appear on a television talk show in New York City. And either she decided, or someone decided for her, to stay and do the talk show. So she missed Woodstock. She wrote a song about it, but she missed the experience. She did the careful thing and the compliant thing, but she didn't do the necessary thing.

And I didn't want to make the same mistake.

I was standing in front of a person, with the possibility of getting to know that person better, and I said, "What were we talking about?"

"My beret."

"Right. And Rex."

"And your ankle."

I stood on one foot to indicate that my ankle was back to normal, and it was almost a conversation. The words were going back and forth like a conversation, but in the back of my mind was a memory of who I used to be, or the almost magnetic pull of who I used to be, and because who I used to be never seemed suave enough or attractive enough, I tried to be someone who would be those things. I rose up off my hips to stand a little taller, and when I did, although I felt physically better, there was still the matter of talking. We were supposedly having a conversation, and I didn't know what the person I was trying to be would say, but she was encouraging me, nodding and talking. And I was staring at her, at her cheekbones and her slightly crooked teeth, staring at her face like staring at an object, a sculptural object. And I guess I was paying so much attention to the visual aspect of her face that, at some point, some neurons stopped firing. The soundtrack of the world got turned off and the event I was witnessing, an event I was part of—the two of us talking—became, in my mind, a silent movie. I could see her mouth talking and smiling, but

41

with the audio part of the program cut out, because I wasn't distracted by the content of what she was saying, I could look at her and feel what I actually felt about her.

This is what I call the realization-that-something-is-necessary-but-not-knowing-what-that-is stage. A necessary thing is any action that makes sense of a given circumstance, that follows naturally what came before, like water flowing down a stream. If you can imagine water, cascading over rocks, actually thinking about something, then what that water is thinking about is the necessary thing, and the beauty of the necessary thing is that it's true to itself, and by being true to itself, it knows exactly what to do.

Which is why I began acting like Scott—like Scott acting like Steve Martin. I was trying to be like water. When I said, "I wish I had a bone for Rex," I said it in a way Scott would have said it, as if I was hearing Scott in my ear and he was telling me what to say.

"He likes toys," she said. "You know . . ." and she made a squeezing gesture.

"Squeezable."

"Right."

And we continued like this, and I guess it wasn't so much what we said, but the way I was feeling when we said it. We moved over to the corner of the store, by the window, and I kept hoping I'd remember something about Steve Martin, or the way Scott had acted like Steve Martin. Being Steve would be a way to woo her, and I was hoping, by thinking about Scott, and at the same time focusing on the present moment, that Scott's carefree persona would appear in me.

"So," I said. "I never asked you. About your past."

She just looked at me, and by way of explanation, told me the story of King Minos of Crete. The story is about how the wife of King Minos used to watch the prized bull prancing in the field. She liked that particular bull and she wanted to have that bull, so she built, or had built, a huge wooden cow, a hollow wooden cow, and one night she slipped inside the cow so that when the bull mated with the cow, and came inside the cow, she was inside the cow. And the offspring of that union was the Minotaur, half human and half beast.

"That's interesting," I said.

Whatever had happened in the past, I thought, that was in the past, and the two of us, standing by the floor-to-ceiling window, we were in the present. And sometimes two people can talk and that's all it is, and sometimes they can talk in a way that moves through the metaphorical skin of the conversation, into the muscle and nerve and the actual joint, and that's where we were going. The more we talked, the more successful the talking seemed to be, and the more I let Scott have his leash, that's the expression. I gave myself over to Scott's imitation of Steve, and it was fun, like play, as in "child's play," and I was carried away with its pleasure.

In New York you can be standing on the street, and without much effort, somebody says something and suddenly you're in some conversation. I'd been in Los Angeles almost a week, and I'd tried to have conversations with people, but aside from salespeople and waiters, nothing was very substantive. But this was. Steve seemed to be working like a charm, and when I say *charm* I mean, for instance, that when I noticed her hands were a little weatherworn, I didn't mind because I didn't think Steve would mind. And maybe I momentarily worried that I wasn't being completely authentic, that in imitating Scott I was being false or dishonest, but how could I argue with pleasure?

She asked me if I had a business card, and I did, an old one from New York. I borrowed a pen from the sales counter, crossed out my New York information, wrote in *Jack*, and circled my cell phone number.

"You might not feel like calling," I said, and she asked for a second card, and she wrote her phone number on the back of that and handed it to me.

"I already have your number," I said.

"Now," she said, "we both have no excuses."

"So," I said, "I guess that's it," meaning "I guess our conversation is over." Although I didn't want it to be over, I didn't feel I could keep up the façade I'd put in place. I was afraid that who I was would eventually appear and that I'd say something or do something to ruin the rapport we'd started to establish.

So I shook her hand. And I noticed, when I did, that she had a good solid grip. When she walked away, I was still feeling the sensation of that grip. I pretended to be looking for a book, but I turned around in time to see her walking past the glass windows of the store.

And then I drove back to the Metropole.

I parked on the street, walked into the lobby, and to the right of the registration desk people were sitting around the television set, watching a movie. It was *Sunset Boulevard*. I stood by the wall, watching one of the old familiar scenes, and then I got my key and went up to my room. I turned on my radio, lay back on my thin mattress, and pulled out the card she'd given me. I was listening to the news about the current war, looking at the way she'd written her name on the card, reading the name on the card, over and over.

Before the actual outbreak of the Second World War a number of people in Europe had felt the erosion of freedom, and the threat of that erosion. A number of them came to Los Angeles, including Billy Wilder, who, in 1950, made *Sunset Boulevard*. In the story, William Holden plays a scriptwriter living in Los Angeles. In an early scene he's sitting on his bed, typing on an old Underwood typewriter, and because his scripts haven't been selling, when he hears his doorbell ring, he knows what's happening. The lending company, in the form of two central-casting tough guys, has come to take his car, and as he says, losing a car in Los Angeles is like getting your legs cut off. So he sneaks out of his apartment, down to a shoeshine parking lot where he gets in his old convertible. As he drives along Sunset Boulevard the henchmen, in their black sedan, chase him through parts of Los Angeles that, like a kind of memento mori, are still topographically recognizable. At a certain point, he feels his tire blow, and he makes a sharp turn into a driveway that leads to an old, seemingly abandoned mansion. We see the black sedan drive past the entrance, and the soundtrack, which was frantic before, now changes to something more adagio. William

46

Holden can relax now, and when he does he notices an empty swimming pool. He's standing near this pool when a voice calls out to him to come upstairs. The voice is the voice of Gloria Swanson, a silent-era movie star, who at that moment is conducting an elegant funeral for a pet monkey. She thinks William Holden is the monkey undertaker, and somehow, the way Holden plays it, it doesn't seem that strange. His character is average and weak, but still morally responsible. He happens to be down on his luck, and by *down on his luck* I don't mean that the henchmen were going to kill him; his situation is only partially about the threat. Mainly it's about the seduction proffered to remedy that threat. Holden finds, in that faded mansion, a kind of utopia. It's handy because he needs a place to stay, and so he stays a few days, and a few days turn into a few weeks, and after a while he and Gloria Swanson begin to play the parts of people being in love.

Jane and I weren't in love exactly, but I could imagine the possibility. That's why I went to Scott's office, in what he called the Old Bank of America Building on Ivar. He was going to become Steve Martin and I was going to see how he did it.

He'd warned me the office was small, and it was, a corner room on the ninth floor with windows that looked out over Hollywood Boulevard and the flat expanse of city beyond it. Against one wall there was a metal clothes rack, and against the other wall was a long folding table. A small mirror was facing the single chair, and tucked into the frame of the mirror was a photograph of Steve Martin taken at some award ceremony.

"I would've thought you'd have more pictures," I said.

He was sitting at the desk, looking at me in the mirror.

"To inspire you."

"I like to keep it simple," he said, adding that his Steve was more a sketch than a painting.

He was preparing for an appearance at an Orange County car dealership, and I was watching his transformation. I watched him trim his white hair with a small pair of scissors. I watched him apply foundation makeup to cover the rough patches on his skin. He used the bathroom down the hall to brush his teeth. And because Steve Martin was nothing if not a sharp dresser, Scott had several suits hanging on his rack. He chose a gray one, then slipped out of his pants, and when he got the suit on, and got the tie tied, it seemed as if the person inside the suit was someone who was happy.

"It doesn't seem that hard," I said, and he grinned his grin.

When I asked him why he didn't change his clothes in his house, he said that he didn't want to confuse who he was with who he was trying to become. And when he said the word *become*, although I noticed the change in his voice and the change in his posture, he was talking about more than physical resemblance.

"The job is to make people happy," he said, and again he used the term *being Steve*. "When I'm being Steve," he said, "I have to forget about myself."

I thought I knew what he meant because every so often I forget about who I am. Usually, when I do, I like it, and as I watched Scott, or Steve, whoever it was, as I saw the transformation in him, I wanted to learn a little bit about how that transformation happens. With Jane, at the bookstore, I felt something, and I asked him about his posture.

He tilted his hips slightly. "Can you do that?"

I tried moving my hips.

"Pretend you have a tail," he said, "and you're trying to get the tail between your legs."

I tried to do what he was showing me, and he must've seen my interest because he suggested I try on one of his suitcoats. He picked one out and handed it to me. And when I got it on, I thought maybe he would want to put some whitening agent in my hair, but he didn't bother with hair color or makeup. He started to show me what to do. He said the important thing was the walk. He showed me an easy, beginner-level version of the Steve Martin walk.

At first I swung my arms in a goofily exaggerated way, and he told me not to try so hard. He told me I already had some Steve in me and . . . "There," he said. "You're beginning to get it."

And it was strange. Although I knew I looked nothing like Steve Martin, as I paced back and forth, I couldn't help smiling, and it felt like the smile Steve Martin would smile. With the suitcoat and the walk and the role model in front of me, I was beginning to feel, slightly, like dancing.

"See what I mean?" he said.

He had a Steve Martin twinkle in his eyes, and I think there was probably a twinkle in my eyes too, and looking into his eyes, I would have to say I liked him. And I did see what he meant.

He told me to forget about the actual Steve Martin and to concentrate on one particular aspect of my own personal Steve.

"Like?"

"Breathing."

And it's funny, because when I'm very relaxed,

usually lying down, I can sometimes feel my body breathing. And it's pleasant at first, but then the same thing always seems to happen. I'm observing my breath, breathing out and breathing in, and it's all fine until, after a while, I start to get worried about who's doing the breathing. Theoretically, I know it happens on its own, but when I try to just let it happen without me, I start to worry that maybe it won't happen, that I'll forget to breathe. And in a similar way, being Steve, even to the tiny extent I was doing it, was making me worried about where, if I was Steve, was I?

"Breathe," he said.

And I did. And when I concentrated I was able, for the most part, to put the habit of myself on the back burner. I was talking to Scott and watching myself talk to him, thinking that if Jane liked the Steve Martin I'd done before, then I would get better. And that's what I tried to do. Instead of worrying about being myself, I could worry about something else.

We talked about girls and families and where we used to live. He said he used to live with someone in Tucson.

"Tucson is dry," I said.

"It's a desert."

"True," I said. "But in a good way."

He told me he'd come to Los Angeles to be an

actor, and that doing the Steve Martin thing had saved him at first but now it was getting in the way.

"Of what?"

He didn't say, and maybe it was getting in the way for him, but for me, although whatever transformation was happening to me was minimal, there was an emotional component, a giddiness in my body that I liked. Although Scott was a better Steve than I was, I wasn't terrible. And I was enjoying it. "That's the main thing," he said. "Enjoy it." And I was. Certainly more than being myself. Which was weird. As if now, because I was this other person, an entirely new world was possible.

I looked at Scott in the mirror and I could see the two of us, reflected in the mirror, my face and his torso, and I realized that Scott, standing there, was a version of what I wanted to be. And because I wanted to be the only version, when I took off the coat I said to him, "You're right."

"What?"

"It's silly. Being Steve Martin? Come on."

"Not being."

"Whatever."

"You're doing a great job."

"Not me," I said. "You. You said it gets in the way and I can see, I mean . . . You've got some girlfriend, right? Waiting for you in Tucson."

He hung up the coat.

I continued talking about Tucson, and got him talking, about Tucson and Los Angeles, and about not having enough money, and I think I saw the twinkle in his eyes start to flicker. We kept talking, and after a while I didn't care about the twinkle in *his* eyes because I had my own twinkle now, and when I said to him, finally, "It's kind of stupid, right? Being someone else," he was looking out the window. And I didn't say anything more and he didn't either, and that's how we left it. When he went to his gig at the car dealership, I didn't tag along.

I finished the look-alike article, and before I gave it to Alan, I was going to show it to Scott, to see if he had any changes. So I drove to his house, and because the people who owned his house didn't like cars parking near their driveway, I parked by a school down on Wonderland Avenue. I walked up the street, knocked at his door, and when he didn't answer I looked through the window next to the door. I could see he wasn't in the "living room" area, but maybe he was in the bathroom, and if so, I thought I'd give him a few minutes of privacy. I walked back down to the school play-ground, looking for his car, in case he'd gone out for some milk or something. When I got to the play-ground I stood on one side of the chain-link fence, watching the kids, running after each other and hiding from each other, and as I was standing there, watching them, I noticed a man coming down the street. He was the kind of person I classified as a bum, a man with a large box on wheels filled with furniture and bags, and because there wasn't any sidewalk, he was walking in the street, near the gutter. He had two Labrador-type dogs on leashes, and when he looked up he said, "I'm just walking," as if I was some kind of security guard.

"I'm just standing here," I said. His dogs were brown and large, and I told him they looked healthy.

"They live outside," he said, and he said "outside" as if it meant, not just outside a house or outside a neighborhood, but outside society, free from the poison of society, and because I must've looked like a representative of that infected society, he kept on walking.

He walked down the street and I walked up the street, and on my way to Scott's house I came to an open area in the hillside. Scott had mentioned a trail, and so I turned and followed it, a single-file trail that wound around what looked like olive trees, and ended at a flat shaded area marked off with stones. Scott had told me about a picnic spot and now I was standing in the middle of it. It was a rock garden nestled in the trees, with a rusting metal chair in the dirt. Near the chair was a cactus plant with a fruit growing on the end of one of its arms, and I knew some cacti were edible, so I plucked off, first the flower, then the fruit. I peeled away the thin thorny skin, and although I'd never eaten a cactus, I bit into the orange flesh. And it was good. It was sweet and juicy and I ate the rest of it, letting the juice run down my lips.

By then I figured Scott had had enough time to do whatever he was doing, and when I came out of the trees and onto the street a man was taking out his garbage. I knew that Joni Mitchell had once lived in the area and I asked him if he knew where Joni Mitchell's house was. He didn't. He said he knew where the Mamas and the Papas had lived but I wasn't interested in the Mamas and the Papas, so I walked back, up Scott's dead-end street and up the steps to his door. I stood in the mottled light, and when I knocked this time it was obvious he hadn't come back, and probably wasn't still in the bathroom, and since I thought I knew him well enough, I tried the door. I turned the handle of the door and oddly, it wasn't locked. The door swung open and there was his room, too small to walk around in, but I stepped inside.

"Scott?"

His bed was made. Pictures were on the walls. His cell phone was on the edge of a fake wood dresser and I picked it up. The place had a definite scent, like the odor of old men, sweet old men, and I liked it. I felt a kind of familiarity, and I'm not an expert on the chemistry of the human body, but I know certain chemicals are released by the body that cause us to feel certain things. And I'm not saying Scott had released any chemicals, but I was feeling the effect of something in my body.

I sat on his bed, looking at the various reproductions of art on his walls. I hadn't noticed them earlier, but I knew Steve Martin collected art, and there they were. A Vermeer of a girl standing by a light-filled window. A print depicting an atrocity of war, by Goya. There were several landscapes by Brueghel, a short-legged jester by Velázquez, and a snapshot of a woman standing somewhere in the sun. Mostly they were postcards, a collection of reproductions he was attracted to.

The desire to collect art begins with attraction. There's an urge to be near a thing of beauty, and over time, when you're with something like that, with something beautiful, a relationship begins to form, and that relationship begins to have a meaning, and it's meant to. A work of art is meant to have an effect, and it does, and the original desire changes from simply wanting to be near that beauty to wanting to possess it, wanting to be so close to it that some of the beauty rubs off.

I remember reading about a museum, an athenaeum on the East Coast, in Connecticut, in which some paintings had been stolen and the curators had left, on the walls, the blank spaces where the paintings had been hanging. People would come and stand in front of the empty spaces on the walls, reading the descriptions, and even without the actual works of art, I think some of the people probably felt something rub off.

Scott's bed was a futon with a quilted comforter on top, and since I was already sitting on the bed, it wasn't hard to swing my feet up over the end of the bed. I rolled over, opened up the comforter, and then rolled back into the center of the bed. Settling into the indentation where he'd probably slept, I covered myself with the comforter, put my head on the pillow, and either the scent of his scalp or the scent of some shampoo had been absorbed by the pillow. I was aware of the scent and aware, in an abstract way, of the lingering electrical trace of a human body. And not just Scott's body. I was lying, face up, thinking about him and also about Jane, wiggling on or against the soft mattress, on or against the soft pillow, trying to lose myself and at the same time absorb both the scent and the life that scent represented. It was warm in the room, and I was warm, and I lay there for a while, burrowing into the warm bed, as if a life, or a desired life, could possibly rub off on another person.

I'd walked down the hill, back to the school playground, and I was just getting into my car when my pocket began to vibrate. My cell phone, I thought, but it wasn't mine, it was Scott's, and I answered it.

"Scott?"

"This is a friend of Scott's," I said.

"Is Scott there?"

"Not at the moment."

The person talking was Scott's mother. Her name was Alice and she'd heard of me, apparently, and mentioned that she was coming to his house to gather some things together. She said she was looking forward to meeting me, and when she hung up, since there was no point calling Scott, I put his phone back in my pocket, and about a half hour later a car pulled up, right into the driveway, right in front of the main house.

Ed and Alice were the sort of parents you'd see on a rerun television show. Ed was heavy and gray, and Alice looked like a woman who'd been sexy in her youth, and a hint of the starlet had stayed with her. She seemed years younger than Ed, who, I could tell, wanted to have a smoke.

"Did he get off all right?" the mother asked me.

"You know Scott," I said.

"We all know Scott," she said, and as we walked up the stone walkway, Alice told me about Scott's decision to go away, and that he wanted his books delivered to him, which was why they were there. They'd driven down from Santa Barbara and I think they were hoping to catch him before he left. But all they caught was me.

"Would you like the royal tour?" I said, and I led them into Scott's cramped quarters.

Alice commented on the beauty of the neighborhood and we talked about Scott's car and about how long it would take to drive to Arizona, and in answering questions about their son—they seemed to think I was close to him—I almost seemed to be taking on some of the attributes of their son.

Ed didn't have much to say. Once they'd gotten a tour of the inside of the house, he was content to sit on the bed reading one of Scott's books, a photography book about Chaco Canyon. Alice and I walked outside, onto the deck, and when she looked over the railing she pointed to the bottom of the canyon and said, "What's down there?"

"Nothing," I said.

"Scott told me about his tunnel."

I told her that there was poison oak down there, but she said she wanted to explore. With me. She asked if I would join her, and I could see she was intent, so "Yes," I said, and we walked down the steps, along the garage and into the dirt. There wasn't actually any poison oak, so we walked down through the dry grass, and although she held my hand now and then, she was agile, leading me down the slope to the entrance of the tunnel.

The ground was wet, and it was slippery, and I didn't know what she wanted to do or see. I didn't have a flashlight, so I poked my head into the opening of the tunnel, adjusting my eyes to the darkness, looking through to the light at the other side.

"This is the place," I told her.

"He's an impulsive person," she said, and she stepped to the entrance of the tunnel, bent down to look inside, and I think she was about to start walking into the tunnel, but because of the mud she slipped. Her feet flew out from under her and she landed on her hip.

"I'm all right," she said, but she didn't get up.

I had been thinking about water, and although I knew that water wasn't capable of thought, I imagined the thought process of water flowing down a stream. And in an effort to be more like water I reached out. Alice was on the dry, sloping side of the rivulet, and fortunately she was what they call petite. I bent down, and because she was light, I was able to lift her, and holding her in my arms, I carried her up the hill. As I climbed up the trail I talked to her, this person in my arms, and when I said to her that she was "light as a feather," it wasn't so much what I said as how I said it. Like Scott. Like Scott doing his impression of Steve Martin. I was talking like Steve, which to her must have sounded like Scott, and she seemed to respond to that. By the time I got her, cradled in my arms, up to the deck, Ed had brought out some folding chairs, and I set her down on one of those.

I went inside Scott's room to get her a pillow, and I noticed the television was turned off. I remembered the movie I'd seen playing on that television when I first met Scott. *Detour* was a low-budget black-and-white B movie from 1945. The director, Edgar Ulmer, had come to Los Angeles from Austria, and the main character in the movie is a man who changes who he is. In the beginning he's a piano player, working at a lounge in New York, and he's in love with a singer at the lounge, a girl who's also in love with him. When she moves to Los Angeles, he decides he can't live without her, so he follows her, hitchhiking his way across the country. He has almost no money, and when he's picked up by a man in a luxurious convertible he thinks it's his lucky day. The man, whose name is Charles Haskell, is driving all the way to Los Angeles, and our hero can finally relax. And when Haskell asks him to drive it's not a problem. The problem happens when Haskell, because he's had either too many pills or not enough pills, falls out of the car. And dies. In this particular scene it's raining, and our hero, standing over the wet body, doesn't know what to do. He didn't kill Haskell but he knows he'll be suspected of killing him, so he leaves Haskell's body in the weeds along the road. He leaves the body but he takes the wallet, and with it, Haskell's money and identification.

I was worried my impersonation of Scott would be too obvious, but no one seemed to notice. Ed volunteered to scramble some eggs on Scott's hot plate, and as a kind of family, the three of us ate scrambled eggs together on the deck. I could hear birds singing in the trees, and as we chewed our food I imagined a measure of happiness in this family, a family that consisted of Mom and Dad and not me, and not Scott, but Steve Martin. He seemed to come up from somewhere inside me. And partly because he didn't seem to be hurting anything, I let him come. And as I continued to be this unreal thing, this made-up thing, it seemed more and more like a natural and generous thing. As my own behaviors began falling away, I noticed that I was liking Ed and Alice more than I thought I would, and especially Alice, who, whatever her age, hardly seemed like a mother. When we washed the dishes, she stood very close to me, and I think she was comforted by my talking like Scott and walking like Scott, and I could have stopped. I could have held myself in a way I considered "like myself," but I could see it was making Alice and Ed, not quite exuberant, but Ed was looking around now at the trees, and the expression on Alice's face was almost as if a veil had been lifted. She kissed me in a motherly way, on the lips, and then I walked them to their car. They backed out of the driveway and drove off, and when they did, along with a certain happiness, there was a vague inkling, a physical feeling that something was still unfinished. Like the man who becomes Charles Haskell. Even if he believed in his own mind that he was Haskell, or even if he convinced a few other people, eventually he would have to prove it to the world.

The following day, in the afternoon, Jane was sitting at an outdoor coffee shop on Main Street in Santa Monica. We'd agreed to meet, and she was waiting for me, thinking about me and what I meant to her, wondering what we were doing together and whether a relationship with me would actually work out. And what that meant, *work out*. She'd lived with a man once, a painter, and that hadn't worked out, and she was thinking about the painter and the life she'd planned with him when I arrived.

I walked to her table and was about to join her when she stood up. "Ready?" she said.

"Sure."

And that's when she noticed my hair.

That morning, in preparation for our "meeting," in an attempt to look a little more like Steve Martin, I'd changed the color of my hair. I'd stood in front of my bathroom sink, opened a packet of hair dye, poured the powder into a bowl, added water, stirred it up into a paste, and now here I was.

"Wow," she said, "you've turned gray."

"It's white, actually."

"It's silvery," she said, and I could see she wanted to touch it.

"It's permanent."

"No, of course, it's just . . . I like it."

And I think she *did* like it.

We started walking, past clothing stores and home furnishing stores, our arms occasionally touching, and although I had the white hair, which *signified* Steve Martin, I didn't feel I was embodying Steve. And how could I? Who was Steve to me, or me to Steve? There were hundreds of actors I could've been, people who had charm and savoir faire. Johnny Depp, for instance, why not be him? That was the question. And the answer was, I wasn't him. And although I wasn't Steve Martin either, that was the possibility that had presented itself.

"You look wiser," she said.

"Must be the hair."

"You're prematurely gray."

"I guess so," I said.

If necessity is the mother of invention, then the father of invention is possibility, and walking with Jane along the sidewalk, watching her eyes glance over at my head, although I didn't say anything about the actual Steve Martin, I was practicing my version of the Steve Martin walk. It was a cross between dancing and staggering, and the trick was combining the two. In the interplay between control (the dance) and loss of control (the stagger) there was a kind of grace, or I should say there *could* be a kind of grace.

"Where do you want to go?" she said.

"Go?"

"Do you want to go to the water?"

"Sure," I said, and although I was talking to her, I was distracted, not only by the Steve Martin walk, but by the whole Steve Martin body. I was trying to imagine a tail at the end of my spine, and walking with this imaginary tail dangling between my legs.

"Is your ankle bothering you?" she said.

"No, no," I said. "I'm fine," and we crossed the street and the cars all stopped for us.

Not only did I have the Steve Martin walk going on, and the tail, but Scott had told me to imagine that my eyes were like ray guns, that a beam of light was shooting out of them, and I didn't know what I looked like, but Jane was looking at me—sympathetically— as if I was having some kind of problem. And the problem I was having was that, although I was enacting the physicality of Steve, the person who was doing the enacting was me. I couldn't quite get into the full Steve groove because there was another groove. I was real, and the groove of who I was was real, and yes, I could picture Steve, with his joie de vivre, walking down the street with a beautiful woman, but because of my idea of reality, I couldn't step into that picture.

When reality and the fantasy of reality are not in complete correspondence there's usually awkwardness, and I was being awkward and she was no doubt noticing, which is why, probably, we weren't talking. We walked past slightly run-down houses and apartment buildings, and when we hit the beach we turned south, walking along the cement boardwalk, past the denizens of Venice, the homeless or almost homeless, and then we walked out onto the sand. We wanted a dose of nature, or at least an approximation of nature, and we walked across the soft sand to an empty lifeguard tower and sat, our backs against the tower posts, facing the waves. I watched her hands moving through the sand, holding the sand and then letting it drain out through her fingers.

A concrete jetty stuck out into the ocean to our left, the hills above Malibu were there to our right, and in front of us was the water. And the waves. I don't know about Jane but I was watching the sky, and the clouds in the sky, and the water, hoping the water, such as it was, would inspire me to jettison the person I still was, the person that was merely imitating Steve. I was sitting there, thinking of a witty question that would engage the two of us in conversation, when I heard a voice.

"Check it out, check it out."

It was coming from the concrete jetty. A small figure of a man in a hat was standing on the jetty, looking in our direction, motioning people to join him.

"What do you think?" I said.

"Let's check it out."

As we walked across the sand I knew I was only being Steve halfway, but I figured half Steve was better than no Steve, and Jane, I think, could tell I was trying. She was not insensitive, and she must have appreciated even my half-successful attempt because she took my hand and we walked onto the jetty. When we got to the end of the jetty, there he was, a normal-sized man in a sleeveless wetsuit, holding in his arms a cinderblock. He had a pair of handcuffs around each wrist; they were attached to a steel cable running through the cinderblock. He had a smudged tattoo on his upper arm, and he was saying "Check it out" to the assorted people at the end of the jetty. He looked at Jane and he said, "I'm the new Houdini."

Although he was talking to Jane, I stepped forward.

"I'm going to escape from the lake," he said.

"The lake?"

"The water, whatever."

I thought there was some kind of trick involved, and since no one else spoke up, I suggested he tell us what it was.

"There's no trick," he said. "I control my body. My body is my vehicle."

I noticed that his hat was now lying upturned near the railing, and I anticipated the payment he'd expect for performing his trick. I started to turn away, but Jane held on to my hand. She wanted to watch. And it occurred to me that this fellow, who had jet-black hair and looked nothing like Steve Martin, was acting more like Steve than I was.

"Feel how heavy this is?" he said, and he held out the cinderblock.

"Why not just tell us the trick?"

"It's not a trick," he said. "I've spent years of my life training for this."

I looked at Jane, who was looking at him, and when he said, "If I could do it with a simple trick . . ." I stepped forward. I placed my hands underneath the cinderblock and yes, it was heavy, and I said it was heavy. And when I did he climbed up onto the railing. He stood there, holding the cinderblock with one hand, the lamppost with the other, his white toes curled over the edge of the railing, looking out to the water. About six people, tourists with windbreakers and kids with skateboards, had formed a circle around him, waiting for him to jump. He was standing there, hyperventilating, getting psychologically prepared, and the water was choppy that day, so I was surprised that when he did finally jump, in the place where he jumped, the water was smooth, like glass. We looked over the edge to see if we could see him, but all we could see was the water, like a mirror.

We were watching our reflection undulating on the surface of the water and then we saw the kicking. His legs were kicking just below the surface, breaking up the mirror, and I thought this was a signal that he was about to come up. He was kicking and kicking at the surface of the water and then the kicking stopped.

I assumed this was part of the trick, to create suspense, and so we waited. The sun got lower in the sky, the skateboarders rode away, new tourists replaced the old tourists, and we waited. And while we waited, while he was gone, down there under the water, it seemed to me the ripples of water radiating out from the place where he jumped were more orderly or more beautiful than I'd noticed before.

And that's when his head popped up.

And the funny thing was, when his head popped up I felt happiness and sadness. I was happy and sad. I was happy that he was alive. And I was sad; he was still alive.

 The meeting to discuss some changes to the look-alike story was Alan's idea. I'd shown him my finished article and he'd given me directions to a spa in Culver City. Although the place referred to itself as a spa, it was really just an old bath-house with some private rooms. I walked through the glass entrance doors into the lobby where I told a woman behind the desk that I was waiting for my friend. She looked on her clipboard sheet, called over an older man with a towel around his neck, and he led me down a wide hall, around a corner and into a room. There was a tub filled with bubbling water and a place to lie down, and at the moment Alan was coming up from under the steaming water.

"Ahh," he said. "You've arrived."

I took off my clothes, folded them neatly on a wicker chair, and stepped down the steps into the bubbly water.

"Don't feel the water," he said. "Let the water feel you." That was another side of Alan, from when he used to spend time at Esalen.

"How long have you been in?"

"Are you letting it feel you?"

I let myself relax a little, sliding farther into the water.

"Now it's feeling you," he said, and he took a breath, and for a moment he disappeared under the water.

When he came back up I thought we would start discussing the look-alike story, but before that could happen he declared he wanted a massage. And he wanted me to have one too. He used the word *massage*, but every time he did he raised his eyebrows as if trying to make that word mean something else, and I didn't know what it was supposed to be meaning exactly, but it appeared to mean more than merely some therapeutic kneading of muscle and skin.

I told him I needed more time with the look-alike revisions, that the subject, meaning Scott, was intriguing me, but the article needed work. "Don't be afraid to finish," he said, and ducked his head into the water. It was difficult carrying on the conversation because Alan kept ducking his head, occasionally telling me that I needed to grease my wheel, and that there was something he wanted me to see.

"See?" Everything was beginning to have quotation marks at this point, which often happened with Alan. Things became "things" and good became "good," and I could almost understand that, but sometimes there were quotation marks around the quotation marks.

"How's your friend Alison?"

"Fine," I said.

"I see," he said, but instead of looking at me, he started giggling, telling me he'd met someone named Betty. He raised his eyebrows again when he said the name Betty, as if to indicate that Betty was more than a name, as if "Betty" was something he knew about, which I would also want to know about, shortly.

There'd been a choice when he booked the room, whether to have a communal room or a private room, and I didn't know why he'd wanted a private room until he stood up, stepped out of the water, and put a towel around his waist.

I was soaking in the warm bubbles, and I could feel the cold air flowing into the room when he walked out the door. And I could see, when he came back, that he wasn't alone, that a short, dark-haired girl was holding his arm. She arrived in her blue bikini. He introduced her as Betty.

I was nude and he had the towel around his waist, and when the girl in the small bikini sat on the edge of the tub I lowered myself deeper into the water. Alan tossed the towel, got into the tub, and I could see what his idea was.

Steve Martin made a movie version of *Cyrano de Bergerac* in 1987, and the basic plot was taken from a play by Edmond Rostand. In the play, Cyrano is in love with a girl named Roxane, but she is attracted to a handsome, age-appropriate soldier. So Cyrano becomes the voice of the soldier. He, the poet, tells the soldier what to say, and speaking through this other person, but using the emotions he's feeling, he woos Roxane. Because his love for her is true, and because the honesty and sincerity of that truth is obvious, Roxane falls in love. She falls in love with the words, and because the words are coming out of the mouth of the soldier, she thinks she's in love with the handsome soldier, but really she's in love with Cyrano. The two stories end differently but the basic plot is the same.

When Steve Martin starred in the movie version, he played opposite Darryl Hannah, a one-time mermaid who now played the part of a scientist. Because of his monstrously long proboscis, Steve Martin (as Cyrano) doesn't think he's attractive to the ladies, and when the handsome, strong-jawed soldier—in the movie he's a firefighter—enlists his help to woo this scientist, Steve Martin (as Cyrano) is torn. But he proceeds. And the ruse works. Darryl Hannah falls in love with the handsome man, but as the wooing continues, Cyrano falls more and more in love with her, a woman he's separated from by his own dissembling.

That's what Alan was trying to do with me. Even though I was the writer, he was trying to be my Cyrano.

Betty quietly slid into the tub and took off her bikini top. She was sitting beside Alan, across the tub, but the next thing I knew Alan was scooting over to my side of the tub so that her round face was facing the two of us. We watched her across the roiling water, and it's possible she enjoyed being watched. Every now and then she let her body float up to the surface of the water.

Then Alan whispered to me, "Your boobies are sweet."

I looked at him as if . . .

"Just say it."

And because I knew what he was doing, and because I wasn't interested in doing it, when he said to me, "Your tits are fantastic," instead of saying that, I told Betty she was lovely.

She smiled.

Alan whispered in my ear, "You look lonesome over there."

What Alan was proposing was that I change my behavior, for just one moment, to let go of who I was.

"Your body rocks." That was Alan prompting me.

I shook my head and smiled at Betty.

"Come on, Jack Man," he said. "Indulge me."

"No way."

"Please?"

"Alan here thinks you're quite attractive," I said to Betty. "There."

"Ask her what she's wearing."

I was pretty sure she could hear what Alan was "whispering."

"Ask her if she's getting hot and bothered."

"Hot and bothered?" I asked Betty if she liked the water.

She smiled, said something about the water's buoyancy, and floated up a little higher, her foot rising up into the bubbles between us.

"Just say, 'You turn me on.'"

"You turn him on," I told her.

"Not me," he said.

"Not him."

"You."

"You're turning on everyone," I said to her. And that's when Alan told me to keep talking. "Keep going," he said, and he closed his eyes. I looked at Betty, who seemed to be enjoying herself, and Alan was enjoying himself, and I'm not saying I was even attracted to Betty, but the idea of doing something that wasn't like me, what was so bad about that? What was so great about authenticity? I'd come to Los Angeles to be something different, and whatever failures and defeats, whatever unfulfilled expectations I was leaving back in New York, that was one thing, and this was an opportunity. To take a step forward. Whatever I would say to her, I knew she wasn't going to mind, and I expected something to come out of my mouth.

Bubbling water was the only sound I heard.

And you could say I was stuck or paralyzed, or that I was in a knot. That's what it seemed like at the time, and what I thought of as a way to get out of the knot was Steve Martin. He would be able to say something. He was just a guy, I told myself, not that different from me, but that difference, when I started to think about it, seemed huge, like a canyon, and I was standing on the precipice of that canyon, and I thought I was ready to jump. I was telling myself, Now. Speak, trying to will myself or trick myself into speaking, scanning my body for a desire to speak, for Steve's desire or any desire, and there comes a point in the progression of desire when, if it's not acted on, it disappears.

"Fuck it," I said.

And I don't know whether I said it like Steve or not, but that's when Betty smiled again. She smiled, and I smiled at her, and Alan started whispering in my ear again. And so I said things. I knew she didn't believe I was actually thinking the thoughts coming out of my mouth, but she seemed to pretend. And we talked, or rather Alan talked, through me, and she smiled, and that was how the conversation worked. In my ear and out my mouth until it became too obvious that whatever I might have been saying, Alan was the one who was thinking it. And feeling it. And since Betty didn't move and I didn't move, Alan

77

couldn't help himself. He floated back to where he had been sitting, next to Betty, his lips mumbling some palaver into her seemingly disinterested ear until, after a while, disinterest turned to interest, and that's when I got up, got dressed, and drove back to my hotel.

There was no chair in my room at the Metropole, so I took off my shoes, sat on the bed, and read my book about the 1947 production of *Galileo*. According to the book, Laughton spent three years working with Brecht on the script, letting the seed of Galileo incubate in him and expand in him, and as opening night drew near, he was feeling the pressure of that expansion. Acting, for him, was a way to release that pressure, and he imbued the characters he played with life partly because it was *his* life he was portraying, and because it was usually an aspect of his life that was hidden from him, it often came out with a strange kind of intensity. Once, when asked why he acted, Laughton said, "Because people don't know what they're like and I think

I can show them." And although he was sometimes accused of overacting, if you knew him you trusted him, and trusted that the place he was taking you, no matter how strange, was probably recognizable.

The Buddhists have a concept called anatta, which translates roughly as *no self*, and as I understand it, after sitting on a cushion for a while—a long while—thoughts and feelings begin to have a clarity. They might come, but they also go, and since they're the things that make us who we are, when they're gone, it's easier to change who we are. And it took a while, but at some point Laughton discovered that he could change who he was into Galileo by putting his hand in his pocket. It seemed strange, even to him, but actors need a trick, and during rehearsals, and even during breaks in rehearsals, he would walk around, his hand buried in his pocket. It didn't matter about authenticity because he was an actor, and being an actor he was happy to empty himself and exchange his own thoughts and feelings for the thoughts and feelings of Charles Laughton. Someone described what he did as an "unconcealed fumbling with his scrotum." And maybe he was playing with himself, or maybe he was playing Galileo, imagining Galileo's surrender to the inquisition, imagining the self-loathing that followed. And maybe *because* he was playing with himself he was able to become someone else and see that yes, here was a great man, and the great man was probably scared.

 I was getting to know Jane and to know we liked each other, and it was getting to be the time, if I had desire, to show it. We met that morning, in the parking lot of the La Brea Tar Pits. We arrived together, parked next to each other, and kissed when we stepped out into the air. We wandered over the wet grass to the largest of the black pits, sat on a bench, and drank hot chocolate from a thermos top. Jane was sitting there, looking into the black pond, and at the edge of it we could both see the tusks of animals raised in a sculptural re-enactment of prehistoric struggling.

"They're huge," one of us said.

"They're mammoth."

"They're woolly."

"They're made of cement."

"Now. But at one time they were woolly mammoths."

That was us, talking.

Because the sun was shining, we were happy to be walking from pit to pit, and we found ourselves leaning against a fence near another pit when a workman appeared. I asked him a general question about the composition of tar, and by way of an answer he invited us into an enclosure. It seemed almost illegal, with all the fences and equipment, but he'd probably worked the La Brea beat for a long time, and he led us through a chain-link gate to a large pit in the middle of some excavation. He pointed out the makeshift cement stairway that led down to the ooze where they'd actually been digging up fossilized remains. He left us alone, and we descended the seven or so steps, and it was warm down there, and oily, and the smell was sweet, like the odor of a railroad track.

We squatted on a large stone, looked into the black pool, and there was something that looked like a skeleton fragment stretching up through the dark viscosity in front of us.

"Is that a bone?" she said.

"It's an animal bone." And then, trying to say it more like Steve would say it, I said, "A dead animal bone."

We'd read that the tar pits were discovered when Los Angeles was still farmland, and she said something about a tar pit catching a moment in the middle of life being lived. And preserving it. "Thousands

81

of years ago," she said, "animals were hunting and mating on this exact spot."

I thought about the wife of King Minos of Crete, and while I was thinking it she stood up.

We walked back up the steps, and we were standing on the grass, breathing the regular air when she said, "Next time we should have a picnic."

"What would you bring?" I said.

"A friend," and she looked at me. That's nice, I thought, and she laughed. And in the expansiveness of her laughter I felt included and encouraged, and I wanted to take whatever distance existed between us and make it disappear.

But it's funny how the body, having learned a way of being, doesn't like to give it up. I was sure that being Steve would make it easier to be with Jane, but often, in the actual act of talking to her, I noticed Steve sliding away. I would make an effort to go back, from my old self back to Steve, and I would go back and forth, and sometimes I got lost in my old self; some memory or fantasy would lead to a series of memories or fantasies and then, like waking up, I'd think, Oh, here I am, and I'd go back to practicing Steve. Not only did I prefer Steve, I was seeing my old self as a hindrance. Which is why I invited her home.

Home, of course, meant the Metropole, and because visitors weren't allowed, we decided to drive our separate cars to her house. She would probably have liked the crowd that hung out in the Metropole lobby. They were all men, all of them quite polite. Earl, who was behind the desk most of the time, was an intelligent guy who was usually reading, and a few nights earlier I told him about the Houdini I'd seen. Earl knew a little bit about Houdini, and he said he considered him, not an escape artist—escaping was the easy part—but a performance artist. According to Earl, his artistry was his ability to make people feel empathy, to feel the possibility of escape. And as I drove down Sunset, stopping at the stoplights, I was thinking about Jane and also thinking about Harry Houdini, inside a coffinlike box, under some body of water, bound with chains and handcuffs, and what if he couldn't break free? I pictured him holding his breath in the darkness, a minute going by and then a second minute, and his chains not coming off. He knew he could only hold his breath for so long, so instead of getting nervous, he did what he'd practiced doing. He'd practiced slowing down his heart and that's what he did, and once he slowed it down, once he could feel his heart's steady beating, he stopped struggling. It's the oldest trick in the book. He stopped trying to escape, and once he gave up trying, his hands easily slid through the handcuffs.

By the time I got to Jane's house, she was already there, straightening up her bedroom. We moved into her kitchen, cooked tomatoes and garlic, which we ate together, and afterward we sat together on her beanbag chair. At a certain point I looked at her and she was talking to me, and as I watched her talk it happened again, the sound got turned off. Not metaphorically, but actually, in my brain, some chemical or electrical signal had paralyzed that one particular sense door. As she talked I could see her lips moving, and I had an impulse to kiss her lips. Her and her lips. And usually I didn't act on impulses like that but this time I did. And kissing usually leads to something, and I remember she said, "Kiss my tummy." And when I bent down and lifted up the material of her shirt, there was her belly button, and around that, her skin, and my lips were following the contours of her skin.

I was in a kissing mood, and she was too, I guess. It was Tuesday, and as the day turned into evening, and as I kept making my eyes into beams of light, and imagining a tail between my legs, being Steve seemed to be getting easier. What I needed to do I seemed to be doing, and sometimes I forgot what it was I was doing, assuming that Steve was me, or I was Steve, and as the kissing continued I found myself feeling desires that weren't normally my desires. But they were there, and when we went into her bedroom she took off her pants and shoes and got into bed.

She lay down on her side, pretending to be asleep. I took off my clothes—everything but my underwear—and as I slid up along her pretending-to-be-sleeping body I could feel the muscles of her back against my chest, and her thighs and her hips and her breasts, which were smallish, the same color as the rest of her skin. It occurred to me that there were experiences she'd had, that there were things she probably liked, and I began thinking about those things. A moment earlier I'd been feeling desire, and now, instead of *feeling* desire, I was thinking about desire, her desire. I was running my hand along her waist and over the rise of her hip, and I could feel her moving. I could feel her pressing up against my groin, and I could hear her breathing, and I could smell her, and all of it, including her wiggling, was an indication of her desire, and her desire was for something to be different.

"Are you all right?" she said.

"I'm fine," I said. "How are you?"

"I'm fine too," she said, and maybe she was.

Because sex is a kind of utopia, it demands that something be different. And I wanted to be ready for that difference. I was desperate, in fact, for something to be different, and I would have reached out and embraced that difference except that something in me was still unwilling. And it wasn't about Jane. And it wasn't about the difficulty of being another person. It was almost as if I couldn't stand the possible happiness that being another person might engender.

The next day I went to a yoga class on the ground floor of Alison's building, in Santa Monica. Since she lived right there, and since I needed a shower, I stopped by. We'd had a period of flirtation in New York, when Alison was a costume designer, but somewhere along the line we'd decided that what we had was friendship. Now she was working in the movie business and I was in her house, standing next to photographs of her as a child ballerina, telling her about my Steve fixation and my idea to find work as a Steve Martin look-alike. I was surprised that instead of some ironic dismissal, she went into her walk-in closet and came back out with a camera. She told me that I would never in a million years look like Steve Martin, that the best I could do was be charming like him.

"That's what I'm doing," I said, and I showed her my walk.

According to her, the walk was acceptable, but she didn't like the hair. "Is it supposed to be so white?"

"It's silver," I said.

"Does it wash out?"

I tried to explain about Scott and his hair, and although I knew that being Steve had nothing really to do with the color of my hair, it was part of me now, and—

"Fine," she said, and she held up the camera. "This can be your head shot."

So I stood in front of the white wall next to her kitchen, and the beauty of the Steve Martin walk is that you don't even need to be walking. I was just standing there, brushing back my hair with my fingers, and everything was fine until, as she started taking pictures, I realized that some tertiary muscles in my face, without my doing anything, seemed to be tensing. She kept telling me to relax and I kept telling her I was trying to relax, but I couldn't forget about the camera long enough to remember what relaxation was. Until she lowered the camera. Then I looked at her in her white blouse. Then it was just the two of us. And that's when she snapped another picture.

"Wait," I told her. "I wasn't ready."

"Doesn't matter," she said. "It was good."

"But that was me," I said, and I suggested she take another, better photograph, but she said she didn't have time.

"We have to get dressed."

"For what?"

"The party."

She had an invitation to a movie "wrap" party, and so we drove our separate cars to the Los Angeles Athletic Club. We found places to park near a Scientology center, across Hollywood Boulevard, met her friend Sharon at the entrance, and because of Sharon's connections we had no trouble getting in.

We drank red drinks in plastic glasses and wandered into a ballroom area and then into a smaller room where tables were set and the crowd was more well-dressed. People were milling around, clustered in groups, and in one of the groups I noticed the actress Scarlett Johansson. Actually, Alison pointed her out. She was the female lead in the movie, and partly because she was surrounded by people, and partly because we'd seen enough close-ups of her face, we were staring. Alison was commenting on her low-cut emerald-green dress, and I wasn't commenting, but I was noticing her red lipstick, which made her look like a version of Marilyn Monroe. And that's when Sharon said she'd be happy to introduce us. She was talking to me. She said Scarlett was really very friendly.

"That's perfect," Alison said. "She can be your new girlfriend."

"She's just a person," Sharon said, and she took my arm. "Come on. Let's go say hi."

I hesitated, but eventually I finished my drink, and with Alison watching, I followed Sharon to where Scarlett was standing, flanked by a group of admirers. They were mainly men, actors and producers and writers wearing glasses. Scarlett was smiling at them, and as we waited in a kind of line, I worried that Scarlett might actually know Steve Martin and would think I was doing a clumsy, second-rate imitation of someone I wasn't. And then Scarlett looked up, saw Sharon, and her smile, if possible, got even bigger. She obviously liked Sharon, and so we approached.

"I'd like you to meet my exceptionally cool friend," Sharon said, and Scarlett turned to me, and she must have been a very good actor because I actually believed she was happy to meet me. We shook hands and then someone named Mandy came over, a friend of Sharon's from South Africa, and because Scarlett had been shooting a movie in Cape Town, they started talking about Nelson Mandela. They all said, "How, are, you," in what I guessed was a Nelson Mandela imitation.

While they talked, I looked back and saw that Alison had gone. She'd stayed out as late as she had for me, and I was thinking I should thank her for the invitation, and that's when I realized Scarlett was speaking to me. Because I was thinking about Alison, I didn't hear what she said, but I looked at her. I noticed her teeth, which were perfect, and her chest, which was pushed up and perfectly visible. Her hair was done up in a perfect chignon, and I looked at her long green dress with its shimmering sequins, and when I looked up from the dress she smiled.

"So you're friends with Sharon?" she said.

I nodded.

Sharon had started talking with Mandy, and Scarlett had turned her attention to me, and was facing me. "Sharon's great," she said.

And I continued nodding, not because I was agreeing with her—although Sharon did seem like a nice person—but because my mouth didn't seem to be working. An actual movie star was talking to me and I was frightened, partly because I didn't know what she wanted me to do. I had *my* desire, and here was a person with her *own* desire, and instead of basking in the paradise of that mutual desire, I let her desire dominate. And I imagined that her desire was sexual. Because of the way she presented herself I could feel a sexual component to our conversation, and although I knew it was probably my own sexual component, what I did in reaction to that, or in reaction to my fear of that, was imagine myself as Steve. If necessity is the mother of invention, then desire is the mother of necessity, and Scarlett was there and I was there, and because there was nothing between me and the perfection in front of me, I said something.

"I'm sorry we missed your movie."

There'd been a showing of the movie before the party, and I told her I'd heard the movie was excellent. It seemed, as I said this, that I was stepping outside myself, that who I was was standing in one place, and as I took a step forward, not only was I talking like Steve Martin, I was thinking like Steve and seeing with Steve's eyes, and it felt pretty good. I wasn't obviously impersonating Steve, but with the white hair I imagined she might have been thinking, This man reminds me of someone.

Steve was certainly all-American, and wearing the mask of Steve, I felt safe enough to see behind the façade of "movie star" to an all-American, or at least a Danish-American, girl, an intelligent young woman with lovely eyes and soft skin. Although she wore a lot of makeup, I could see through the makeup, and when I did, it wasn't her desire or my desire, it was Steve's desire, and I was ready to act on that desire when she turned. She turned away from me to someone else. I was still standing there, but she turned to

91

the next person waiting in line and she started talking with that person. It was clear our conversation was over, and so I said goodbye to Sharon, and then I left.

It was a beautiful afternoon. Jane and I were walking around an outdoor sculpture park near UCLA. It was the opening of an art show and we found her friend's exhibit, a platform with telescopes and measuring devices, and as we looked through the telescopes, her friend, whose name was Bob Braine, said I reminded him of someone. Since I was more interested in thinking like Steve than looking like Steve, I didn't say anything, and we continued walking around the various installations. The art we saw, although it was both visually and even philosophically pleasing, wasn't very emotional, and since we were both feeling the need for some emotion, we were happy when we came upon the movable wall. An artist named Dave Wave had built a thick steel wall in the middle of the lot, and the wall was movable. If you pushed on it, it moved like a gate. Various people were pushing on the wall, but because they were on opposite sides, the wall wasn't moving. We watched them, and when they left we started to do what they'd been doing. We stood behind the wall, on opposite sides, and when we pushed, because we were pushing against each other, of course the wall didn't move.

"Let's try something," I said, and I walked over to Jane's side of the wall. We both stood on that side, and when we pushed, suddenly the wall, which had seemed so intractable, very easily swung open. I mention it because, metaphorically, that's what we were doing. That's why we drove, in our separate cars, back to her house.

Once inside we moved, by habit, into the kitchen, where the light was. She said she wanted to make me a meal, and I said that sounded excellent, and then she started cooking, risotto and mushrooms. While she was chopping, I wandered out to the patio, where Rex was sleeping on his rug. I was standing near her sliding glass door when she said, "There's more backyard around the side. I thought we would eat inside, but . . ."

"No, inside's great."

She let me stir the risotto, and the beauty of risotto is that, over time, because of the constant stirring, you can actually witness the beads of rice opening and expanding, taking in the liquid and becoming something else. I demarcate my relationship with Jane from the moment of the risotto. There was the dinner, and then after dinner we moved to her beanbag chair where she showed me her collection of postcards. We were sitting there, just the two of us, and we'd been talking about the postcards and she was about to get up. As she leaned forward, shifting her weight to the front of her body, I held out my hand and she took it and held it as she rose to a standing position. She held it a little longer than she had to. Quite a bit longer, so that I was able to use my hand as a sensing device to feel the warmth of her hand, and the softness of her hand, and the blood that was flowing between our two hands.

Chet Baker was singing his songs about love, and the music was nothing if not romantic. He was singing his songs as if for us, and without ever officially beginning, we just started dancing. I should say I started *trying* to dance, trying to do a good job, but the secret of dancing is enjoyment.

"I'm not normally a very good dancer," I said.

"We don't have to dance."

"No," I said, "I want to."

It seemed like the necessary thing to do, to keep going in the direction we were going. If this was a habit, I wanted it, and so I moved the coffee table out

of the way and we began moving together on the orange rug in her living room.

I was able to concentrate on Jane, and at the same
time I was also practicing Steve. And by *practicing* I
mean not just imitating, I was practicing *being*, and
I continued practicing, noticing my thoughts, good
and bad, and noticing the world in front of me.

At a certain point I realized that trying to dance
like someone else wasn't good for dancing. So I
stopped, turned my attention to the person whose
hands I was holding and whose body was pulling, and
being pulled, by me. And with Jane I seemed to be
light on my feet, or at least lighter than normal.

"You're light on your feet," she said.

"You think so?"

We were holding hands and I was twirling her.
That was something I could do. Twirling was fun, and
we were having fun doing it, dancing as if in a movie,
an old movie, a black-and-white movie starring Cary
Grant.

Later, we were sitting again on the beanbag chair,
drinking tea, our hands curled around our separate
mugs. Billie Holiday started singing a song about
love, singing that love was "like a faucet, it turns off
and on . . ." And I was like a faucet, or Steve was a
faucet, something was a faucet and I didn't care what
it was because, looking into her eyes, her head lean-

ing against the soft pillows, her face turned toward mine, I felt desire, and I didn't examine that desire to determine if it was my desire or Steve's desire. It was just what it was, and I held her midsection in my hands, just below her ribs, and we started kissing.

Walt Whitman famously said he contained multitudes, and I knew what he meant because as desire expanded in me, Steve also expanded. I could feel it happening and I was letting it happen. We were squirming around each other, into each other and through each other, in a multitude of ways. And then she led me to the bedroom.

I was acquainted with her body now and knew a little better what she liked, and what I liked with her. I knew how she liked to be touched and kissed, and we touched each other and kissed each other, and I knew her neck was sensitive. She pulled her sleeveless shirt up and over her head. Her bra came off and we were still wearing socks. I felt like kissing her breasts, so I did. I unbuckled her belt and we pulled, first her pants off, then mine, and I was in my underwear and she was in hers, and Here I am, I thought, with a beautiful woman, and then the thought disappeared. Or more accurately, it became Steve's thought. Lying in bed, our faces half buried in our pillows, I realized that my desires and Steve's desires were the same, that I'd been merely resisting—for whatever reason—the reality of these desires. I was looking at her half-buried face, and the thing I'd been trying to be, now without trying, I was.

 You sometimes hear people say, "Take the bull by the horns," meaning face some dilemma and act, which was what I was doing, going to the office of Scott's agent and trying to get a job as an actor. In my own opinion I was a pretty good impersonator now, and if I could get paid for it, why not? I had the number of the casting agent, and I called her, arranged an audition, and there I was, sitting on a purple sofa, thumbing through the current issue of *People*.

I'd created what I called the art of continuous Steve. Not being Steve for just a moment, but being a nonstop Steve. It had required effort, and I'd put in that effort. And when I was called into the casting director's office I stood up off the purple sofa, trying to retain some fruit of that effort.

I was led into a large room where a large woman framed by large windows was sitting behind a large desk piled with papers and photographs of actors' faces. Bonnie, the casting director, was talking to me and I was sitting in a comfortable chair trying to make a good impression. I kept repeating her name, saying, "Well, Bonnie," or "It seems to me, Bonnie," hoping that the repetition of her name would facilitate some rapport. Since this was an audition, I suppose she was getting to know if she liked me, and so we talked. I told her about the traffic on my drive over and she told me about Scott, that he'd called her from Tucson and that he might be staying there for a while. And then she asked me to do my thing.

"Thing?"

"Make me laugh."

"Ahh . . ." I said. "That."

"Isn't that what you're good at?"

I could see she was looking at my hair, and I explained that although my specialty was Steve Martin, Steve wasn't always funny.

"Just give me a sample," she said. "You know . . ." and she moved her hand to indicate that I was free to do anything I wanted.

So I sat up in the chair and started talking. I forget about what because the important thing was Steve, and I talked with a come-what-may, devil-may-care joie de vivre that seemed to me quite charming.

"You do other things too," she said. "Right?"

"Yes," I said, but in my mind I was thinking no, that I don't do other things, that Steve is what I do. And because she was waiting for me to do something, and because I wanted to do something, not knowing what else to do, I said, in a Steve Martin version of a Nelson Mandela imitation, "How, are, you?"

Audition comes from the Latin, "to hear," and the Steve Martin accent I heard coming out of my mouth sounded good to me, but Bonnie was there to make money, and since there weren't that many calls for a Steve Martin impersonator, although she was looking at me in a sympathetic way, I started to worry. Alison had told me that my neck was too long, that I should wear a shirt with a collar, and I think Bonnie was looking at my neck. There was no way to shorten it so I tried to relax. I knew that relaxation was the key, but how could I relax with the desk, and the head-shots on the desk, and my neck.

"You are intense," she said, and then she closed her eyes. I assumed she was trying to visualize me. As something. I didn't know what it was but when she opened her eyes she said she had an idea. She was casting a crime show and they needed a serial killer, and she thought I might be good at that kind of thing.

"Really?"

"Give it a shot," she said.

When I lived in New York I tried my hand at writing screenplays, and in an effort to get better at writing for actors I enrolled at a theater school. It was famous at the time, and before you were permitted to take a class you had to have a one-on-one orientation session with the teacher. Mine took place in a small room with miniature chairs, like kindergarten chairs, and I sat on one of these chairs and the teacher, a woman with muscular arms, told me, "Repetition is death." She said, "Whatever you do, you have to feel it like it's the first time because I want to sit on your face each time is the first time or you lie to yourself and you start to rot inside, and then you die, and that's why repetition is death."

She looked at me as if she hadn't said what I thought she'd said, and so I said to her, "What did you say?"

"Repetition is death."

"No. Before that, you said something."

"Whatever you do, you have to feel what it is for the first time."

"No. You said something else. Something . . . You said . . ."

"Repetition is death. Repetition is death." She kept repeating, "Repetition is death." And yes, it was weird, but really she was a very good teacher, because after I'd left the room and was walking down the street, and even now, years later, the only thing I remember for sure that she said was, Repetition is death.

Bonnie was looking at me, sitting behind her large desk, not as formidable as she'd seemed before. I was in one of two chairs facing the desk, and I remember standing up, looking out, past her gray or slightly purple office, to the sky outside the window. I'd spent so much effort making my life become Steve's life, and here was this person giving me the freedom to change that life, and although I knew that repetition was probably death, because Steve gave meaning to my life, I was stuck. When I tried to imagine how I could act that was different than Steve, I couldn't. And that's when it happened. That's when I became aware of emotions bubbling up in my body, and one of these emotions was resentment, at Steve. Steve, it seemed, was constraining me, and the longer I stood there, not moving, the more I felt the constraint, and with it, the resentment, hardening, turning into anger, and then into something like hatred, and although these emotions were directed at who I was, I was looking at Bonnie. And as I stared at her, in her swivel chair, it occurred to me that these emotions, and an inability to change these emotions, might be a key to the psycho mentality.

There I was in this situation, standing near the corner of her desk, and although I remember standing there I also remember watching myself stand

there, thinking about repetition, and death, and instead of doing something obvious, instead of yelling
at her or attacking her or howling at her, the thing I
felt like doing was to hold it all inside. To feel like
howling and not. That's what a serial killer would do,
and that's what I felt like doing, and I watched myself,
very slowly, approach her. I was whispering something, not to her but to me, to the serial killer that
Steve had morphed into, and although I was hiding
it, a certain amount of havoc must have been seeping
out. I must have looked as if I might break the civi-
lized constraints of our little "audition" and do something crazy. I won't go into what I was imagining
doing to her but it was crazed and deranged and from
her look I could see that she was actually frightened.
Of me. And that's when she told me she'd seen
enough. "That's great," she said, and I looked away.

I was still standing by the corner of her desk. I
was letting the anger, which had been liberating, dis-
sipate.

"Very nice," she said.

And it took a while. My heart, I realized, was still
beating away, and it took a minute before it slowed
down to normal and the regular everyday Steve came
back into my body.

She nodded, said something like "Well, I'll be
keeping you in mind," and when she stood up to

shake my hand it wasn't awkward, but there was still some lingering tension between us. Which was good for getting a job, but as I rode down the elevator, and as the lighted numbers above the door moved from right to left, I noticed that the part I'd been temporarily playing, just moments ago, didn't seem to want to go away.

Brecht had begun writing his *Life of Galileo* during the rise of fascism, but I think the play, at least partly, refers to any ideology that tells people what they can and cannot be. And by *ideology* I mean especially the personal ideologies that we use to "believe in life" or "give meaning to life," or make it possible to "be yourself."

Brecht came to America around the time of the Second World War, when the United States, which had been basically an innocent country, found itself with an ideology. Suddenly American soldiers were passing out cigarettes to European orphans. Suddenly power had been transferred to a culture that wasn't used to power, and didn't have the experience of power, and to the émigrés it seemed like a possible utopia. At least it did to Brecht, who came to Los Angeles because of the safety and because of the climate, and also because of the movie business. He had friends in the movie business who kept telling him there was money to be made. But Brecht had seen enough repression in the world, and the ideology required to support that repression, and although the abundance of Southern California must have been intoxicating even to him, he knew that protest was necessary.

This was around the time the atomic bomb made its debut in Hiroshima, and as Brecht and Laughton worked together on the translation of *Galileo* they talked, in broken English, about theories of acting and theater, and also politics. Brecht tried to instill in Laughton the idea that repression demanded protest, and that acting could be a form of protest. And although Laughton respected Brecht, and although he was aware of repression and the falsity fostered by repression, whenever he tried to protest he got stuck. It always seemed to be a protest against himself. Even thinking about it made him anxious, and every so often he would say something like *"Ich muss ein break getaken,"* and shuffle over, past the grandfather clock, and sit on the white sofa. Brecht, in his journal, remembers him reposing, "legs crossed so that his

Buddha-like tummy was visible." I picture them in a large library, with a fireplace, a grand piano, cigar smoke swirling in the air, and Laughton declaiming the lines of Shakespeare's not-quite-human Caliban.

> *You taught me language, and my profit on 't*
> *Is, I know how to curse.*

One morning, while Jane and I were lying on her bed, in her room, in the morning light, Rex wagged his way into the room. We were relaxed and warm and wound around each other, and she kicked off the comforter. She got up, fed Rex, made coffee and toast and blueberries with yogurt, brought it to the bed on a wooden tray and we talked about where we wanted to go that day.

"Where do you want to go?"

"I'm still hungry," she said.

It was after noon by the time we finally got up and made lunch.

I chopped watercress and she made an omelet, which ended up being more like scrambled eggs, and after we ate I was ready for a nap. She said she was ready for a nap, but she'd been neglecting Rex. Rex had been wagging his tail all morning and she felt guilty, so we leashed him up and headed for the park he loved. I loved it too. It was another cloudless day, and we took a different route than the last time, and this time we stopped at a playground area with swings and pull-up bars. We took off our shoes and she stepped on my cupped hands, reached the highest bar, and immediately began doing some Olympic routines. That's what it seemed like to me. She was able to swing on the bar, building up enough momentum so that when she sailed off the bar she landed on her feet.

"Impressive."

"I was a gymnast."

"You're tall for a little gymnast."

"Little?"

"I thought gymnasts were little."

She rolled up the cuffs of her cotton pants and did another trick, and this time when she landed I deducted points for her dismount. She said she'd nailed the dismount, and then she pushed me and I pushed her and we stayed in the sandpit, playing around the bars, and then we played a game in which I was supposed to catch her, which I did.

The effort of being Steve didn't seem necessary anymore. It was happening on its own, and when she began swinging on the swing, I started pushing her, thinking the whole thing was very romantic, like a Watteau painting but without the greenery and the flowing petticoats.

"You're a boy I knew in grade school," she said.

"I remind you of someone."

"No. At this moment, you are him."

"Was he big?"

"You have an obsession with size, I think."

"Do you picture him as an adult, or as a twelve-year-old?"

"You're spoiling my reverie," she said.

I liked that word, *reverie.* "You know what my reverie is?"

I paused to savor the air and the distant sounds of traffic. The metal swing was almost singing as she swung.

"This," I said.

We put our shoes back on and walked up the grassy hill where she pointed out a Japanese garden with pools of water. There was a chain-link fence separating us from the camellias and cypress trees and pristine pine trees. Orange fish were swimming in the almost rippleless pools.

"This is idyllic," I said, and she pointed to a rustic wooden bench overlooking one of the ponds. She was in the middle of telling me how great it would be to sit on that bench when Rex, who'd been sniffing around behind us, suddenly ran into the grotto. He'd found a hole in the fence and ran through the hole and into the quiet calm of the garden. Running wasn't Rex's forte, so there must have been something he was running after, and from the perimeter of the garden Jane was calling him, "Come, Rex. Good boy," pleading with his obedient side, but Rex was already deep into the bamboo thicket.

"I'll get him," I said, and I started to climb the fence. I was going to be the hero, I thought, and when I got up to the top I looked back and Jane, who was also climbing the fence, was having some trouble with a foothold. She was having trouble getting the toes of her shoes to fit between the links in the fence. So I climbed back down, gave her a literal hand to put her foot on, and once she was on the fence I climbed back over and gave her a hand to get down on the other side, the Japanese garden side.

And there we were, inside the place where weddings happen, and in this sacred (or semi-sacred) place Rex was acting like a wild beast. Jane was calling out, "Rex, Rex," desperately trying every tone of voice she thought would work, and for an overweight dog Rex moved very quickly. He ran past us, teasing us, and at one point we thought we had him calmed down, corralled in a corner, but that just made his excitement greater. That's when he jumped into the pond. Suddenly the smooth water wasn't smooth anymore, and the orange fish that had been swimming disappeared.

I was worried that, like muscles going back to their old familiar positions, the Steve I'd been successfully being was only temporary, only there when the proverbial sun was shining, but even in this emergency, Steve's muscles were my muscles, and I could feel those muscles taking a new and unfamiliar direction. I could feel myself getting pissed off, and I knelt on some stones at the edge of the pond, and while Rex was splashing in the water I tried to get hold of his collar. When he paddled away across the water I wanted to jump in after him, and although I didn't want to get my clothes wet, I thought, Fuck it, and I jumped in. The water came to about my crotch but I didn't care because I was running, or trying to run, after Rex, trying to grab his tail, which of course I didn't do.

"Your dog's a little crazy," I said.

"He's not the only one."

Jane was standing on a little bridge and I was standing, crotch-deep, in water.

"You're soaking wet."

"I'm trying to catch your crazy dog."

"By jumping in the water?"

"What do you want me to do? Nothing?"

Rex had disappeared by this time, so I stepped out of the water. And as I did, the emotional muscles which had veered off in a different direction began to return to something more familiar. When I walked out of the pond, back to Jane, I was acting more like a regular Steve. My pant legs were heavy so I tried to wring them out.

Jane was looking at Rex, somewhere in the bamboo thicket, and we stood on the bridge and I could see she was worried. I said, "Maybe we should pretend to leave him."

"You mean use psychology?"

"Dog psychology."

"Okay," she said, and then she yelled out, "All right, Rex. We're leaving now. Rex?" We stood there, listening.

After a couple of seconds I said, "I don't think it's working."

"Rex?" She was begging him almost, to be good.

"We should start really walking away," I said.

"We can't leave him."

"We should *act* as if we're leaving."

So we started to walk back to the fence. On our way we passed the bench she'd wanted to sit on. It was partly shaded. I took her hand and we walked to the flat area around the bench, overlooking the pond, and I sat first. She was nervous because of Rex, and because of disturbing the peace, but I pulled her onto my legs. Since my pants were wet she sat down next to me, on the bench, and as we looked into the pond I could tell she was thinking because she said to me, "You don't have to . . ."

"What?"

But she didn't seem to want to say anything, and I didn't know what to say, so we didn't speak.

In searching for Rex our emotions had run wild, like a dog's emotions, and now, as we sat, and as the confusion settled, we could see through the havoc we'd created to a serene and beautiful paradise. Being Steve was fine. It didn't matter about him because it wasn't about any one person, it was about what exists *between* people. Or between people and animals. Rex was free to run as much as he wanted, but without anything to struggle against, eventually he calmed down, and we hardly noticed when, after a while, there he was, at our feet, happy and panting. We weren't panting, but I think, at least temporarily, we were happy.

I went back to the Metropole, and for the rest of the day I stayed in my room. What I remember is lying on the bed, staring up at the wire mesh that formed a ceiling over my cubicle, slightly below the actual ceiling. It was like a cage, this mesh, and by focusing on it, although I knew the actual ceiling was there, all I saw was the wire mesh. I went back and forth like that, seeing the mesh and then the ceiling beyond the mesh, and then changing my focus again and making the mesh the boundary of my world. I did other things too. I slept and read and went to the bathroom down the hall. From the vending machine in the lobby I got a coffee and some snack food, but by the time it got dark I was feeling like something else.

Not too far from the Metropole was the Japanese part of town, or at least the Japanese part for tourists. There were restaurants and tea shops and I'd found a tiny shop that sold little balls of ice cream wrapped in mochi, which is made of rice. It was about nine o'clock when I walked to the shop, ate four of these mochi balls, and then started walking, through the deserted streets, back to the hotel. The streets weren't completely deserted because, although the cut-rate stores were all closed and shuttered, people were scattered around. Most of them, I think, were homeless. Some were sleeping in or on cardboard boxes, and on the street I was walking along, I came across a man huddled on the sidewalk. He was wearing a plaid coat, and he had shoes on his feet, and he said something to me as I passed him.

I didn't hear the words exactly, and because they didn't seem like violent words or even aggressive words, I asked him what he'd said.

"Slim," he said.

"Slim? You mean I'm slim?"

He was a large man, half reclining, and I could see a green bottle in his dark hand.

He didn't respond to my clarification, and I probably should have just walked on. And I probably would have walked on, but with the hand not holding the bottle he gestured to me. His arm was extended in a half embrace, and so I stepped off the street onto the sidewalk.

"Brother," he said.

"Brother," I said, not knowing what it meant but thinking it meant something to him.

"Brother," he said again. And that's when he looked up and I could see his face. His eyes were red and he was dirty, but his look—first his gesture, now his look—seemed to be a kind of invitation.

"What's up?" I said.

"Up?"

"How are you doing?" I said, and at that, or because of that, he slumped back down and looked at his bottle.

He seemed safe so I squatted in front of him, not too close but close enough to see, when he looked up at me again, that he looked like an American Indian. I was wondering if there was an American Indian population in Los Angeles, and then he scooted his legs up under him and sat against the accordion metal behind him.

At the top of the street there were some voices, shouting, and when I looked back at the man he was holding out his bottle, saying to me, "Drink it."

I wasn't keen on drinking from his bottle, and I suppose I would normally have thanked him and walked away. But what was normal wasn't obvious anymore, and so I stepped up to the metal shutter next to him. The cement wasn't filthy so I bent down and sat, my feet on the sidewalk, my back against the shutter. And then I took the bottle.

"Brother," he said.

"So you say," I said, and I wiped the lip of the bottle and took a sip. It was sweet, a wine-like liquor, and it wasn't the wine, but when I sipped the wine and then looked up, the world that I saw seemed different. I suppose it had been different for a while, but now, sitting there, gazing across the deserted street, I was aware of the difference, not sure what it was exactly, and then the man moved to put his arm around me. When his arm slipped off my shoulder he told me to "drink it."

I told him, "I did drink it," and that's when I heard the voices again, the same loud voices, and I looked up and saw a group of young men walking down the middle of the street.

I could see they weren't bums because their white T-shirts were clean. There were four of them, and it's funny because, although I didn't actually feel any fellowship with them, I stood up. I suppose I wanted to indicate that although I was *with* a bum, I wasn't a bum myself. And when I stood, that's when the young men, who were just about to walk past us, stopped.

They stood together and one of them stepped forward and said, "Motherfucker," and although he didn't use the plural, it seemed he was addressing both of us, me and the man at my feet. "Motherfucker," he said, a little louder this time, and because I was feeling a sense of possibility, and because at this moment protest seemed appropriate, I said, "Are you talking to me?" I didn't say it like some Martin Scorsese wiseguy. I was just asking a question.

"I'm talking to him," the ringleader said, indicating the Indian man to my left.

I must have looked like Steve Martin to them, like a respectable white man, and when I said, "Why don't you keep walking," they were surprised. So was I. And when the one guy stepped forward and said, "Motherfucker," again, I noticed his boots. I noticed all their boots but I didn't really care.

They were looking at the Indian man and I was looking at them, and like electrons vibrating, they seemed to be vibrating, with each other and against each other, and they were exciting each other. I heard one of them mutter something about trash on the street. The word *trash* kept coming up, and then the ringleader said to me, "Back off, Jack."

"What did you say?"

"Back off."

Well, I could tell they were about to do something, and I said, "I don't think so," and I stepped away from the wall.

In any kind of negotiation, including a physical one, the person with the least to lose is the person who has the advantage, and at the moment . . .

"The dude is diseased, man."

"Do you have a problem with that?"

And when the ringleader said, "What?" it wasn't about my words. It was something else, about the way I stepped away from the wall, my arms at my sides. I think they still expected me to be Steve, but I didn't want to be Steve. And I wasn't. At that moment I didn't know who I was, and maybe not knowing who I was, I was going a little crazy. Maybe I wanted them to beat the shit out of me, I don't know.

"I said, Do you have a problem?"

"You got the problem, dude, unless you leave that motherfucker to us."

The Indian man was behind me, curled up in a ball, and I was looking at the kids. They weren't men, they were boys, and I said, "Just keep walking."

"Is he your friend?"

"Yeah."

"He's your buddy, huh," and they all laughed.

"Yes," I said. "He's my brother."

I could see, forming in their minds, a question about what to do. I was ready, as they say, to do battle, and because I was ready, and maybe because the young men could see I was ready . . .

"Fuck you, old man," the ringleader said, as insulting as he could make it sound. Another man said, "Pussy," under his breath, but as they said these things they backed away. Their body language was already turning, and after that their bodies turned, and with as much swagger as they could imitate, they walked on down the street.

I waited until they were well away, watching them and feeling the adrenaline in my blood. And it felt good. Unfamiliar but good. And I didn't expect my new friend to thank me, but I was surprised when I turned to him and he looked at me and he said, "Motherfucker."

This time there *was* aggression in his voice, and That's odd, I thought, and in the split second it took to think that, he must have raised his bottle, because the next thing I knew the pieces of it were crashing at my feet.

The man, who had been sitting, now fell to his side, taking the posture I'd seen him in when he first introduced himself. The street was deserted, as it had been before, and as I had been doing before, I walked back to the hotel.

Sunset Boulevard was shot in a style of filmmaking that was brought from Germany, transplanted to Los Angeles, and flowered in 1944 when Wilder teamed up with Raymond Chandler to make *Double Indemnity*. In the movie, a man makes a deal with a woman, based on their sexual chemistry, to kill the woman's husband. Beneath his hard-boiled shell, the man is a moralist, and by *moralist* I mean he knows what he ought to do but can't quite control what's happening. Chandler was a writer of detective stories who hated detective stories, a drinker who tried to stop drinking, and although he didn't write *Sunset Boulevard*, both movies have a Raymond Chandler aesthetic. Both films show the insecurity behind American optimism, they both deal with femmes fatales, and in both films a character wants to change his situation.

In *Sunset Boulevard*, after living with Gloria Swanson for a while, William Holden decides he doesn't want to live with her. He's ready to leave, ready to get on with his life, but he's "asked" by Gloria Swanson to ignore that life and the facts of that life and live in a Hollywoodland of the past. I say "asked" because how can you refuse the seductions of a benefactor? How can William Holden protest against the strong desires of another person? She wants him to be something, and although he's against corruption in principle, it's easy to tell himself his own situation is only temporary, that he's only temporarily rewriting her ridiculous movie and only temporarily watching her pathetic imitations of Charlie Chaplin. He tells himself he's going to leave, but the fear (of the repo people) and the comfort (of being taken care of) are making him, literally, a kept man, and there's a scene—I'd seen it playing in the Metropole lobby—of Bill Holden and Gloria Swanson driving through the city. It's a two-shot, and he's dressed in an elegant suit that she bought for him, looking at a watch that she bought for him, barely aware of the various streets they're passing, or the stores, or the world that used to be his but isn't anymore. Until Gloria Swanson gives him some money. She wants a pack of her special cigarettes, and they pull up to Schwab's drugstore and she reaches into her purse, takes out a bill—a large bill probably—and of course William Holden takes her money. He has none and she has plenty, and so he takes the money, goes into Schwab's where he meets again the wide-eyed script girl who sees potential in his screenplay. Which gets him thinking. He begins thinking about how he might get free of a situation in which he's found a certain comfort but lost any connection to what he is.

Jane had gone to a café in Los Feliz to see a friend play music. The friend, Eli, was the drummer in a band that played songs for children, and there were mainly children in the narrow back room. The point of the show was to get the kids to dance and sing, and Jane sat close to the stage, facing, not the band, but the children in the audience, the bright attentive eyes and the small bodies hopping to the music. When the concert ended she walked with Eli to the backyard patio, which was filling up with mothers and a few fathers, and children running around a tree. The kids were all different sizes, and Jane noticed a little girl in a white dress, smaller than the others, not quite part of the group but wanting to join the group, and Jane thought to herself that the past is the past and the world does what it wants to do, and that's when I walked into the patio. I was supposed to be there at three, so I was late, and when I saw her I walked to her. "How's it going?" I said, and instead of kissing, she introduced me to Eli, who had curly hair.

A man was standing behind a grill making hamburgers and hot dogs, and I asked her if she wanted a hamburger. There was a salad bowl with plastic knives and forks and Jane said she'd have a salad, so we sat at a table in the shade, Jane eating her salad and Eli eating a veggie burger and I had a hamburger. We talked about the lyrics of the songs, which I hadn't heard, but Jane liked them, and she said, "The one about the ring falling into the ocean should be in a book."

Eli made a self-effacing joke about what he would look like trying to get the ring back, and Jane laughed, and when she turned to me I could tell she expected me to say something equally funny. But I wasn't feeling funny. I was watching the two of them across the picnic table, and I knew, if I wanted to be Steve, I could have said something humorous to make her laugh, and maybe make Eli laugh, but I didn't want to be a trained animal doing a trick, so I didn't speak.

"It would be like diving into shark-infested waters," Eli said, and he began describing himself under the water, flailing around, fending off sharks. And because I wasn't saying anything, Eli, who was enjoying the attention, continued, describing himself talking to the shark and trying to reason with the shark, and what he was saying was funny. He was acting more like Steve than I was, and Jane was smiling at him when she turned to me.

"What about you?" she said. "What would you do?"

"To get back the ring?" I wasn't completely sure what they were talking about anymore.

"What would you do?" she said, and what I did was sit there, remembering the shark cage I'd been in, and how that seemed like ages ago, and how Eli wasn't in a cage and I was. And now Jane was frowning at me. Not only was I not speaking, apparently I'd been chewing my hamburger with an open mouth, something she didn't care for. She waited until I closed my mouth and then she turned back to Eli. It was clear that she was in some kind of mood, and people have moods, I realized that, and she seemed interested in Eli, and he probably felt something about her, and I imagined the mood she was having had something to do with that.

Bonnie got me a job on a television show called *Crime Story*. It wasn't a Steve Martin look-alike job, but it was something that would pay. I was hired to play a small-time thief called "The Leader," who was trying to unload some of his stolen goods at a pawnshop. Luca, played by the star of the show, was a big-time thief who wanted to control the city's racket, and in this one particular scene I'd left my gang and gone alone into the pawnshop. Luca's henchmen had knocked down the pawnbroker and Luca was standing behind the counter. When I walked in I could tell something was wrong.

"Who are you?" I say to Luca.

"We're who you do business with," he says.

His sidekick, Pauly, comes up from the side, sticks a gun into my ribs and shoves me up against the display case.

Luca, with his slick black hair, wants me to sell my stuff to him, at his price. But I have to make a profit, that's my motivation, and I tell him, "I can get a better price."

"Then you don't do business in Chicago," he says, and he steps around the counter in a threatening way.

The director yelled "Cut." He walked up to Luca and me and he said to both of us, "That's fine, that's really great, but . . . you know . . ."

And I thought I did know.

He didn't want two actors acting a situation, he wanted the characters in the script to be real people, engaged in a real struggle. I'd read somewhere that a director is like a lover, and it was true, I wanted to make him happy. My character, as written in the script, was a certain kind of person, and what I think the director wanted was someone to take the character in a new direction. And I was willing to do that.

The next shot was Luca's reaction shot. They moved the camera behind my back and I positioned myself against the counter. Pauly must've been a method actor because, with some force, he jammed his gun into my ribs. And then the cameras started rolling.

"I can get a better price," I say.

Luca comes around the counter. "Then you don't do business in Chicago," he says, and he reaches up and slaps my cheek, lightly. He's improvising. He's the star so he's allowed to improvise. "You got a problem with that?" he says. He's taunting me. "Huh, big shot? You got a problem with that?"

I heard "Cut," and then the director got out of his chair and he was holding his hands together, as if praying. "Yes," he said, nodding, and I couldn't tell if he was nodding at me or at the star. Either way, I knew I hadn't completely become my character, that I'd been thinking too much about the script or too much about the cameras or too much about what I was supposed to do. The director, with his nodding, was offering me the freedom to do what I wanted, and my spirit was willing, and my flesh . . . that was willing too.

In *Rosemary's Baby*, John Cassavetes played a man

who was doing the work of the devil. That, or he *was* the devil, and had taken the form of this man, the husband of Mia Farrow and the father of her unborn child. Either way, the devil wanted the child to be his, and in the beginning, the Cassavetes character tried to fight the devil, tried to protest the usurpation. But the devil was wily. I forget the actual deal he made. Whether it was about wealth or power or fame doesn't matter because what the devil had promised was freedom, the alleviation of the pain of being human. So naturally Cassavetes fell, not in love, but in thrall, with the devil. His choice was between the paradise he imagined (with the devil) and the paradise he knew (with his wife), and although he was probably torn, what was his choice?

I say "What was his choice?" because by the time he knew what was happening, it was already too late. By the time he was ready to choose, he'd already turned, not only against the woman he loved, but against the man he'd been. Without quite knowing it, he'd become the devil's apprentice. He'd started wearing the mask of devil, and now the mask had become his face, and he couldn't take it off. It wasn't a case of "I like it" or "I don't particularly like it." It wasn't a question of the script he'd been given because the devil had given him a new script. And that was who he was.

I'd also been given a script. And the script was fine, as far as it went, but I had my own ideas about what I would do, and be, and when they set the camera behind Luca, looking over his shoulder, at me, I was ready, as they say, for my close-up. I was up against the counter, the gun digging into my rib cage, bruising my skin, but I wasn't thinking about that. They turned on the sound and then they turned on the camera and I thought I knew what they wanted, but I also knew that repetition was death.

"I can get a better price," I say, looking right in Luca's eyes.

"Then you don't do business in Chicago," he says, and he comes around the counter, starts slapping my cheek, harder than before, and he's laughing, "Come on, big shot," slapping my cheek, getting more animated, saying, "You got a problem with that? Huh? You got a problem with that?"

And I say, "Yeah. I got a problem."

He stops slapping me. I take Pauly's arm, I twist the gun out of his hand and I push him away. This isn't in the script, and he doesn't know what I'm doing. But I know what I'm doing, and it feels good. I'm becoming my character.

I turn to Luca. And I've left the script at this point. "You son of a bitch," I say, and I grab him by his lapels. I don't exactly lift him up, but I lift up his jacket, and it looks good from the camera's POV, I can tell. And I look at him, as intensely as I can, hold the look for about a beat, and then throw him into the electric guitars lined up behind him.

I hear the director yell "Cut." I watch him put his clipboard on his chair. He walks over to me, and I'm an actor, and he looks at me like that. And I look at him, like a lover.

"Good," he says. "You were good."

But you can never tell with a director.

A few scenes later the police stormed into a derelict warehouse, their guns drawn, their flashlights shining, and they found me, limp and dead, hanging from a meat hook.

The next thing that happened—obviously not the next thing, but the next thing I'm going to relate—happened with Jane. As part of my introduction to Los Angeles I wanted to see the Watts Towers, and although Jane had seen them she agreed to come along, and so we drove down, saw the various structures and the pieces of broken glass in the structures. We read the booklet about Simon Rodia, who'd decided he wanted to build something, and spent the next thirty-three years making his imaginary city real. And what I want to relate happened after we'd seen the towers and been impressed by the towers and we were walking back to my car.

"Do you want to get something to drink?" she said.

There was a small store across the street.

"Or do you want to go home?"

I was telling her I'd just as soon go home when a man approached us. He was wearing a dashiki and his head was bald and he was carrying a four-by-five camera around his neck. He asked me if I wanted a photo taken. "Of your wife," he said.

"She's not my wife."

"The two of you," he said, and he motioned for Jane, who was standing off to the side, to stand next to me.

"I don't think so," I said. "But thanks."

"Why not?" Jane said to me, and then to the man, "How much?"

He told us one photo was five dollars, or three for ten, and he held up a sample of his work, a photo some previous tourist had probably not paid for.

"I don't want a photo," I said.

I had enough photos, but Jane was already reaching into her pocket—she was wearing shorts—and was pulling out money.

"To remember the moment," she said, and she handed the man some money. I couldn't tell if it was a five or a ten, and then she ran back to me and he positioned us so that the cement-encrusted rebar spires were rising into the air behind us.

"Hold it," he said.

And that's when I had a vision. Not really a vision, but there I was, Jane's arm around my waist and my arm over her shoulder, and I could imagine the frame surrounding us, the rectangular vision of the camera, capturing our knees at the bottom, the air at the top, and the wall made of cement we were standing in front of.

I was Steve and Jane was Jane, and the man said, "Step this way," meaning toward him, and Jane and I each took one step, together. But then I took another step. We were standing on some dry, barely living grass, and when I took that other step, when I lifted my leg, I lifted it high, high enough to step over the frame I imagined across my knees. I stepped out of the frame and moved to the side. "Take it now," I said, "without me."

The man, who had been squatting in the sun, stood up.

Jane held her arm out so that, like pieces of a chain, I would link up with her. She had a picture in her mind and the picture to me seemed false.

"Don't be coy," she said.

"Coy?"

"Stand by the lady," the man said.

They were both urging me to do this thing, and the man looked frustrated and Jane was probably frustrated, and she said, "Jack Cat," and looked at me in a way I thought was extremely coy.

"What?" I said.

But I knew what. It was what she wanted, and it would have been easy enough to do what she wanted except I wanted to do something else. I felt rebellious.

Around 1960, because of bureaucracy and possibly some complaints, the city of Los Angeles wanted to tear down the towers. They were thought to be unsafe, and an inspection crew was called in. It was less inspection crew than demolition crew, because what they did, to test the strength of the towers, was to try to tear them down. Rodia had built them by hand, with rebar and wire mesh and mortar and pieces of glass. All by himself. He'd already moved away by the time the crew came in, attached a metal cable to one of the lattice-like spires, and using the crane, pulled the towers down. Or they tried to. But of course the towers remained intact. They remained intact then, and also later, during the Watts Riots, and except for a little renovation after a recent earthquake, the towers Rodia built are still there.

And I don't remember if I felt like the towers, not moving, or like the inspection crew, unable to make the thing move. Whatever it was, I ended up walking over to Jane. I didn't step up and over and into the frame because I was already in the frame. The frame was a cage, and although it was false, once I was inside it, her arm went around my waist and my arm went over her shoulder. The man focused his camera and took, for five dollars, one picture.

At one point in his career Charles Laughton played the role of Caliban in Shakespeare's *The Tempest*. Caliban is a not-quite-human creature, living comfortably in the only comfort he knows, getting along perfectly well until his island paradise is invaded. A storm comes and a ship lands and Prospero takes over. He was a duke in Italy and now the island becomes his personal dukedom.

He's a magician, and he uses his magic as a kind of technology, giving him power and ownership, and because he has power, Caliban becomes his worker. *Servant* might be a better word, or even *slave*, but in the beginning Caliban is happy enough. In exchange for his work, he's learning a language. And it would all be fine except Prospero has a daughter, Miranda. Although Caliban has never even seen a woman, when he sees Miranda he seems to know what he wants. He has access to her room in the cave, but I think the incident that happens, happens by a pool, a spring-fed pool deep enough for bathing. Caliban is hiding behind some bushes, watching Miranda swim in the pool, and when she steps out of the water, stretching her arms and letting the sun warm her naked body, that's when he stumbles out of the bushes. Miranda looks up, sees him, and Caliban sees her, trying to cover herself with her hands and arms. And because he's not quite human, he acts. He acts on feelings that exist in the pit of his stomach, and in the pit of his stomach he's drawn to her, and he goes to her, and he doesn't know what to do. Except hold her. The urge he has is to press his skin against her very different skin, and when he does, that's when Prospero arrives. And that's when Caliban is imprisoned. There's the actual incarceration, in a cave, and there's also the incarceration of his newly aroused desire, and in response to both of them, rebellion, which itself is a kind of arousal, seems like a necessary thing.

Alison wanted to show me the sights of Los Angeles, and one of those sights was two hours away, in Del Mar. It was Willie Shoemaker Day at the Del Mar racetrack, and when Alison suggested we drive down, since I hadn't spoken to Jane, I agreed. We got to the Spanish-style complex, founded by Bing Crosby and his cronies back in 1937, bought our tickets, walked through the gate, and when a woman gave us each a hat, I didn't think much about it. Everybody had one. Families gathered around snack bars, women holding ice cream cones, and single men with racing forms were either wearing or carrying the green hat, which, although it was honoring Willie Shoemaker, featured the Buick logo.

We weren't actually interested in betting, so instead we strolled to the paddock. We watched the horses, paraded around by Mexican men and an occasional blond woman, and when I turned around, away from the horses, I saw something I didn't quite believe. I tapped Alison on the shoulder.

"Is that Steve Martin?" I said.

A man in a suitcoat, wearing the green baseball cap, was walking across the pavement toward the race-track building. He was with a young woman, her hair in a ponytail, and another man not wearing the cap.

"I don't think so," Alison said.

"I do," I said, and I did. And I followed them.

With Alison behind me I followed them from the sunny area outside, into the actual stadium, and because I was coming from the bright sunlight, when I got into the area where people place their bets, it took a while for my eyes to adjust, and when they adjusted I didn't see Steve.

I walked through this area—what I would call the lobby of the racetrack building—and out to the area in front of the actual track. People were out in the sun, sitting on benches or standing, drinking beer and holding miniature pencils and pieces of paper and I thought, since Steve and his male friend were fairly tall, that I would be able to spot them above the sea of people—that's the expression that came to my mind, a sea of people—and I waded into them, looking at the faces of men in caps but none of them were Steve's.

Alison was still with me, telling me it probably

wasn't him, that the cap made it seem like him, but I knew it wasn't just the cap. I'd seen his face, and more than his face, I'd seen his savoir faire, and at a race-track savoir faire stands out. So I kept looking, thinking about where he might have gone. And since I knew he was rich, I figured he'd go into the expensive seats, and I walked to the stairs that led to those seats. An usher was charging twelve dollars, and I took out my money, paid her, and got my ticket. Alison said she would wait for me there, and I left her and went up to an area that, although there were fewer people and a nicer bar, didn't seem all that luxurious.

More of the people on this floor had gray hair, and there weren't that many caps on heads, but possibly Steve had taken off his cap. So I walked, slowly and methodically, past the betting tellers and across the carpet, looking for a threesome like the threesome I'd seen in the sun. I went from section to section, scanning faces and the backs of the heads, unable to find the man I was looking for when suddenly there he was. Or there I thought he was. He was alone now, in a sportcoat and a green cap, holding the handrail, walking down the stairs. As I ran to the stairs I heard an announcer announcing the start of a race, and I went down the stairs two steps at a time, but when I got to the bottom, although Alison was there, the man was gone. To my left was a large arch with sunlight coming in, to my right was a bank of closed-circuit television monitors. And there he was, standing under the monitors, watching the horses getting into the gate. People were gathering around the screens, their heads tilted up for the start of the race, and I could recognize him because in him I was recognizing myself. "Steve," I said, and I walked up to the back of his upturned head. I don't know if it was the cap or the coat or the gray sideburns, but even he looked as if he was only pretending to be Steve Martin.

"Steve?" I said, and when he didn't turn around I said to Alison, "He looks ridiculous." She took my arm to lead me away, but "No," I said. "Really. Look at him," and I turned to the man. Like a poison in my blood I felt disgust, and I said to the back of his head, "It's pathetic. You're pathetic," I said, but by then the race had already started. People were yelling at horses and shaking their racing forms, and I was talking to him, telling him about his pathetic grin and his pathetic friendliness, and the fact that who he was had mutated into a parody. A parody of a parody. And when the race ended and some horse won, I stepped up to him and I said to him, finally, "You look like an idiot," and of course that's when he turned, and that's when I saw that he wasn't Steve Martin. And that's when Alison, holding my arm, led me, like you'd lead a drunk person, out of the racetrack lobby and into the sunlight.

We walked to an area of grass on the edge of the bleachers. There, standing in the sunlight, I looked around at the assortment of human beings going about their business, some of them walking, some of them standing, some of them sitting at picnic tables. They were living their lives, but the sense I got, looking at them, was that they were dying, that they'd gone about halfway, and now, in the middle of their dying lives, they were trying to make themselves happy.

I remembered a painting I saw in Scott's house called *The Harvesters*. It's by Pieter Brueghel, and in the painting an entire countryside is depicted, and by implication an entire world, with background and foreground equally visible. In the foreground men and women who've been harvesting grain are resting beneath the shade of a tree. It's probably hot, and they're enjoying a lunch break. They might be considered the focus of the painting, except the landscape and the objects in the landscape—the world of the painting—extend far into the distance. There's a church in a valley and people down in the village. We can see them, with parcels on their backs, going about their businesses, and farther away, more people, and beyond them hills, and beyond them the clearly visible mountains. The entire world is there, more or less in focus, and because everything is part of the same world, even if you can't quite see the entire world, you can sense what you can't see in everything you can.

We were standing on the grass, which was clean and soft, and I was tired and Alison was tired, and when she sat, I sat next to her. I took off my shoes and socks, lay back on the grass, and wiggled my feet in the air. She stopped doing whatever she was doing and lay on her back beside me. We were both look-ing up into the sky. I could sense her body next to mine, her cheek and her breathing, and it felt very sane and natural. I could feel the blades of grass press-ing up through my shirt into the skin of my back.

"You know," she said, "you're not some other person."

"I know."

"I thought you were freaking out back there."

"I'm not freaking out."

"I'm just saying."

And I was about to ask her what she was saying, except I knew what she was saying. Because I felt it. I'm not good at looking below the surface—to me everything is below the surface—but Alison seemed to see beneath the surface of who I pretended to be, and by not running away when she saw it, in effect she was saying she accepted me, that I didn't need the security of being someone else, that I had a choice, that I could go back to my impersonation of someone's impersonation of someone I didn't even know, but I didn't have to.

The next day I met Jane at a movie theater, a multiplex on Sunset Boulevard. The site of this particular theater had once been the site of an old Cinerama theater, and I mention it because the history of Cinerama is partly a history of utopia. In the early 1950s television was taking over, and as a way to make movies more popular, the people in charge decided to widen the screen, to make the events on the screen bigger and therefore more real. They thought they were imagining the future, the modern way to see movies, and I was thinking about this when I saw Jane standing behind a glass wall.

I waved to her, walked inside, and the first thing she noticed was my hair. "You have a new haircut."

"Yes," I said, and I did.

That morning I'd gone to a drugstore, bought an electric shaver, stood at my bathroom sink, and starting at the sides, I shaved my head. I adjusted the shaver to leave as much as I could, but I shaved off anything that was white, or silver, whatever it was, working the shaver along my scalp until any hair that reminded me of Steve was gone.

"You could be a Marine."

"It's a buzz cut," I said.

I thought she'd want to touch the short, soft hairs, so I lowered my head, but she wasn't interested. She suggested we go to a café.

That sounded good to me but first she had to use the bathroom, so we rode up the escalator and she went in a door marked with an illustrated woman and I went in the other door. Because the bathrooms shared a common wall, the doors were next to each other, and as I walked to the urinal I was thinking about Steve Martin, but instead of walking like him, now I was trying to walk as *un*like him as possible. I wanted to be with Jane but I wanted to do it as something other than Steve, and since Steve felt good, and since Jane only knew me as Steve, it took some concentration. I stood at the urinal, slumped and uncharming, and as I shook off the last drops, I could hear through the wall the sound of water falling on water. Jane, I was sure, was sitting in a stall on the other side of the wall, peeing, and to me, the fact of our acting on the same impulse at the same moment, connected us. The wall was a barrier, but our urinating connected us *through* the barrier, and this made me feel optimistic.

We drove our separate cars to a café she liked on Sunset, found a table, and I sat across from her, with my back to the window. Couples were together and people sat alone with computers. I ordered tea, Jane ordered a hamburger with french fries, and when our food arrived I raised my mug. *"Bon appétit,"* I said, and I realized I was saying something Steve would say, as if Jane was a trigger for the Steve in me. And in an effort to counteract the impulse of Steve, I changed my posture, slumping a little lower in my chair. The table wobbled, but just slightly, and she said, "Have some," referring to her french fries. She forked onto my bread plate some of her food, and the way she was reaching across the table, with both arms stretched out, was like bridging, or trying to bridge, the distance between us.

"I'm glad to see you," I said.

"You're glad to see me eating, you mean?"

She smiled, and then we both smiled, and behind the smile I could see her vulnerability. Part of me wanted to seem like Steve and assuage that vulnerability, but another part of me, the part I was listening

142

to, didn't. So I didn't, and when she finished eating she stood up.

"Should I follow you?"

She shrugged.

"Where's your car?"

"Around the corner."

And I would like to say that when I walked with her, out of the restaurant and around the corner, I was following my desire, or better yet, that I was following the fruit of desire which is love. I was hoping that her desire would influence my desire, and together our mutual desire would create a space for happiness. I wanted to reach out past all the façades of being, and the question is, How do you do it?

We walked out into the sunlight, into the dry air and the cumulus clouds, and I followed her around the corner and up the sidewalk. We were walking between lawns in front of houses, past palm trees and hibiscus bushes, and when she saw her car she stepped into the street. Holding her keys, she walked to her car, stood by her door, and with a familiar arm-thrown-out-in-invitation gesture, she told me her door was unlocked.

She was talking about her passenger door, and I took a step forward, so that I was standing on thick grass. And let's say I was feeling the buoyancy of the grass through the soles of my shoes. Let's say I could imagine myself, walking across the grass to her passenger door, opening the door and getting into her car. Let's say I was feeling the possibility of Steve, the lightness and buoyancy of being Steve. And as the fractions of seconds ticked by, I was resisting that possibility. I was telling myself that Jane was the real thing, and that this was what I needed, but Steve and Jane were connected in my mind, and because Steve was not the real thing, I continued resisting. I stepped off the grass and crossed between the two fenders and walked to the street where she was standing. She was standing there and I was standing there, and as if we'd been having a conversation, she looked at me and said, "Sometimes I get the feeling you don't really see me."

"I see you," I said. I could feel my heart speeding up. "I'm seeing you now."

"You're *looking* at me now."

"Right," I said, and even as I said it, I realized I wanted to say something else. And I tried to find, in my body, a different response, but it wasn't easy because all I could hear was my heart. No cars were driving on the street so the street was oddly quiet, and we stood like that for another second or two and then she opened her driver's side door.

"Where are you going?" I said.

She looked at me and then she got in her car. She

closed the door, rolled the window down, and looked up. "You're welcome to come."

"I could follow you," I said. "Where are you going?" I kept asking her where she was going, but I knew where she was going. Home. She was asking me to go home with her and that's what I wanted to happen. Or had wanted. But now I wanted something else. I couldn't seem to be with Jane without being Steve, and I decided, at least temporarily, at least until I'd gotten rid of Steve, to let Jane go. I told her about my car. My car was parked in a different residential neighborhood, in a one-hour-only zone, and if I got in her car . . . "I'm in a one-hour-only zone," I said.

"You're not coming?" she said.

"My car."

"Because of your car?"

"I'll call you," I said. "How about that?"

"That's fine. Call me," and then she reached forward, started the car, and I could see our conversation was over. I didn't necessarily want it to be over but now she was waiting for me to stand back so she could pull her car into the street.

Both her hands were on the steering wheel, and although we didn't always kiss goodbye, I wanted at least to seal our affection. Even if I didn't ride with her now, I wanted the possibility of doing so at a later date. That's why I stepped closer. But she was low in the car seat, and when I bent down to the empty space of the open window, she just looked at me. She didn't prepare to be kissed.

"See you," she said.

And then she drove away. She pulled out of her spot, swung into the main part of the black street, and I watched, first her, then the car, getting smaller and smaller until eventually she must have turned, because I lost her in the confusion of all the anonymous cars in the distance.

There was a lightbulb in my room at the hotel, and under the bulb I'd been reading Brecht's *Life of Galileo*, and I'd also been reading a book about Cary Grant. I was especially interested in the period dealing with the late 1950s, during what was called the "Cold War," when his acting career had already peaked, his marriages hadn't worked out, and although his happy-go-lucky persona was famous, it wasn't completely authentic. He said as much when he started taking LSD. That was

146

about 1959, around the time he made *North by North-west*, when the person who called himself Cary Grant was still the apotheosis of charm.

"Everyone wants to be Cary Grant," he used to quip. "Even I want to be Cary Grant," and what he meant, I think, is that the person who called himself Cary Grant was just an actor, a Brechtian actor in the sense that, although he became whatever character he was playing, he knew he was a fiction, knew his elegance and self-possession were make-believe. He knew he was only playing a part, and he knew the audience knew, and because he didn't pretend other-wise, he played the part to perfection. That was his charm.

But charming people can also be deceitful people, and because Cary Grant was really Archibald Leach you could say he was deceitful. Certainly he had a dual nature, but because we all have that dual nature, we trusted him. We trusted him because he didn't completely trust himself, and that lack of trust is why he started visiting a doctor, a psychiatrist, and why the doctor began giving him the then-legal hal-lucinogenic drug. The devil-may-care persona of Cary Grant had become a rut, and first of all, he didn't like ruts, and secondly, although he'd left Archibald Leach in his past, the fact was, Archibald Leach was still a part of him. He felt it beneath the mask of Cary

Grant, and because he was tired of wearing that mask, because he wanted to let his various disguises fall away, he took a glass of water, put the small round pill on his tongue, and swallowed.

It's not hard to imagine him in the specially prepared room at the clinic. It was made to seem like a real room, with real furniture and a real rug. He was sitting in a comfortable chair with the psychiatrist sitting in another chair, and he was feeling the effect of the drug, noticing that both his body and his world were changing. He'd walked into the room with one reality and gradually that reality faded away. And the tendency anyone has, when reality is gone, is to retrieve it and restore it, and I give credit to Cary Grant, or to the doctors supervising him. He stayed in this untethered state, bouncing around inside his own head as the chemical, like a kind of poison, began to work. And as it began to work he noticed the color of the wall and the marks the roller left when it painted the wall, the almost topographical texture, like looking down at a landscape from an airplane. He was looking at the paint, not wondering what color it was, or what color he'd prefer to paint it; he was just looking, at the wall, and the rug underneath his feet, and the socks on his feet, and his hand. The shape of his fingers reminded him of an animal.

It's hard not to think thoughts when someone plants them in your head, and when the psychiatrist began asking him questions about his childhood in England, the thoughts that grew in Cary Grant's mind were images of his mother, specifically an image of her when he was a child. She's lying on her sofa, with doilies and antimacassars, and he's smelled the aroma a thousand times, and he can hear her telling him, "I want you to love me and mean it," and Cary Grant didn't know if he was telling the psychiatrist this, or just thinking it.

In my mind he's sitting there, eyes closed, thinking about what the psychiatrist is saying, and when he opens his eyes, there's the doctor with the horn-rimmed glasses, and he recognizes the doctor, but he doesn't recognize himself. He can feel himself inside his body, and he can feel himself expanding inside the skin of that body, stretching the skin until it finally cracks like a dry shell, and who he is, underneath his skin, stands up. This is me, he thinks, and although he's actually still sitting in the chair, he sees himself standing up. He watches himself take a few steps away from the chair. The person in the chair is Cary Grant, and he doesn't want to do that anymore. The doctor is talking to the chair, or the person in the chair, and he can see himself walking away from the chair, and away from Cary Grant, leaving behind the personality he used to have. He walks behind the chair to a window. It has a venetian blind, and he pulls the cord that pulls up the blind. There's a section of grass outside and a section of street and he unlocks the window and raises it. He can see cars passing outside the window, and he can smell the air, cool and warm, and it seems to him like paradise. He looks back into the room, then he looks out the window, at the possible freedom out there, and he knows he's not Archibald Leach anymore, and he decides he's not going to be Cary Grant.

And most of us profess a love of freedom. In theory, freedom is admirable and desirable, but how do you make it happen? How do you live, moment to moment, responding honestly to the unknown moment unfolding? Freedom is partly about facing the unknown, and the problem is, losing the known, losing the thing we've spent so much time acquiring, is difficult. The doctor is still talking to the person in the chair, and the doctor's a doctor and he's the patient, and he can feel a part of himself wanting to tell the doctor, I'm not Cary Grant. Like someone wanting to protest, Cary Grant wants to turn and climb out the window. And he would, except for one thing. Cary Grant is sitting in the chair, and although he wants to stop being Cary Grant, he enjoys being Cary Grant, and he feels himself pulled back to the chair. He walks to the chair but he doesn't sit. He wants to tell the doctor, "I don't want to sit," but like a child who can't yet speak, he can't yet speak, and all he does is stand there. He stands there until after a while he gets tired of standing, and then he sits. He watches himself sit down on the dark upholstery. He could feel the old mask forming around him, around his face and his body, and although he fit into the form of what he used to be, he didn't feel like what he used to be.

A few nights later I had a dream. In the dream I was holding Jane in my arms, looking down at her, and she was naked and I was naked and the dream was precipitated, I think, by events that actually happened. Bonnie had found me another role. I would be starring—that was her word—in a video, and she didn't say it was a video game, but that didn't matter. It was being filmed in a warehouse downtown, and I arrived in the morning. I parked near a flower store specializing in funeral flowers, found the entrance door where people were bringing in lights and monitors, and where Maria, the assistant director, told me what I would be doing. The part I was to play was the part of the monster.

The video game had a story, and in the story a monster would be wreaking havoc on the citizens of an imaginary town, and the object of the game was to stop the monster by killing it.

I found my dressing room—a barely converted bathroom—and found my red costume hanging on a hanger on the shower rod. I thought it was going to be a monster costume, a gorilla or space creature, but it was just a body suit, made of stretchy lycra. Except for the headgear it was a one-piece outfit, with small photosensitive wafers sewn into the material. I sat on the chair in the bathroom, and as instructed, took off all my clothes, pulled the costume up my legs and over my arms, and when I emerged from my changing room Maria zipped me up. I was completely covered, everything except my face and my feet. Because the floor was cold they allowed me to wear my socks.

The crew was still setting up equipment, so with the costume on, I found the craft service table and stood there, drinking lukewarm coffee. Without the weight of clothes I felt light and springy, and because the bodysuit was so snug I was practically nude. Instead of a monster, I felt like a superhero, like Superman or Spider-Man, and when I looked around the warehouse I imagined looking for an evil deed that would need a superhero's assistance. The warehouse itself was a large open room with lights and several cameras facing a wall covered with blue paper. The images would be shot against this blue screen, and later, when the blue was removed, the images could be placed in whatever context the producers wanted.

The director, whose name was Auggie, patted my back, felt my arm muscles, and told me I was going to be a great monster. "What kind of monster am I?" I asked him, but he was already busy talking to a grip or a lighting person, and when the set was ready I was told to stand in front of the blue wall and then walk back and forth. "In a particular way?" I said, and Auggie told me to crouch, and then to look around as if I was hunting for something. We did this for a while, until the actress came into the room. Her name was Erin, and I could see she was an actress because she was attractive like an actress. Plus, she was the only other person in a bodysuit. We were twins except her bodysuit was white and shimmering, and where I had a cap, she had her hair uncovered. I could see in her long blond hair the electronic wafers that would indicate the action of the strands of her hair.

I was the monster, and my main job was to carry her. When the director told me to lift her up in my arms I nodded to her and she nodded to me and I held her, one arm under her knees and one arm under her back. And because there weren't any townspeople or houses, just the two of us against the blue wall, there was nothing to take my attention away from her, and because my nose wasn't covered I could smell her. She smelled good. Her bodysuit covered her completely, but because it closely conformed to the contours of her body, I couldn't help think, or imagine at least, that she was naked. The lights were bright on her bodysuit, and I didn't want to stare, but there were her breasts, among other things, clearly defined. And the director was telling me to see her, like King Kong would see her, as a prize I'd just taken away. She was my treasure, he told me, and my love, and so I looked at her as if she was a prize, a prize I deserved, a sexual prize even. I was looking at her, thinking a monster would look at everything, at the cleft in her chin, at her ribs sticking out, at her stom- ach and the indentations in the fabric made by her pubic hair. Because I was holding her up, I had a view of her abdominal muscles. I could see her belly going in and out, and although she wasn't what you'd call a large-boned girl, she wasn't petite either, and after a while I was beginning to feel a tension, in my arms, but mainly in my back. And this sensation of tension gradually turned into a sensation of pain, in a spot right about where a bra strap would have been. I tried accepting the pain, or tried trying to accept, hoping that with acceptance the pain would lose its meaning, or at least its old meaning, but the pain must have seen through my trick because it didn't go away.

154

At one point I expressed an interest in taking a break, but I was told the camera person, who always seemed to be in the middle of a shot, was in the middle of a shot, so I never got a break. I was feeling what I called pain, and I knew one way to forestall pain was to find a distraction, and there I was, trying to hold this woman in my arms, looking at her nipples poking through the thin material, and that was certainly a distraction, and the pain partially went away, but what took its place was arousal. I realized I was getting an erection. And the thing was, the erection didn't feel like mine. And of course I wanted it to go away, but as Erin got heavier in my arms, and as she started slipping down my body, the arousal started to intensify. I was reaching down under her body, trying to get a better purchase on her, finding some place I could grip, and the heavier she got, the lower she slid down my bodysuit, and the lower she slid, the more excited my body, which didn't seem like my body, became. She was hanging in my arms, and I don't think the camera could see any telltale bulge in my costume, but if she slipped down any lower she would *feel* the bulge. "I love and hate, and if you ask me why, who knows? I feel it done to me, and I'm torn in two." That's Catullus, the Roman poet, and I think I knew what he meant because I wanted to put her down. And I suppose I could have done that. I could have said, "I have to let go," and let her slip out of my arms, but the bulge had a mind of its own. So I held her right where she was. And the more I held her where she was, the more my back was aching, and there was a battle between my aching back and my aching prick, between putting her down or holding her there, and between the two of them I didn't dare move. I was stuck, and half of the experience was agony and half of it was pleasure, and because of the pleasure I didn't let go of the agony.

In almost any experience there's usually a little agony and usually a little pleasure, and the problem is, happiness is something else. Happiness is a state containing both pleasure and agony, a state that accepts and encompasses and transforms the whole range of experience, and when I called Jane the following afternoon, happiness was what I thought I wanted.

"Do you want to do something?" I said.

"I don't think so."

"Where are you?" I could hear sounds of traffic on her end of the conversation.

"I'm fine."

"*Where* are you?" I said.

She was running errands down on Fairfax somewhere, and I told her where I was, at Alan's house.

Alan had gone away for the day and I was housesitting, taking a break from my room at the Metropole. Since Alan had a reasonably nice kitchen I was going to use it. I was going to make tacos, homemade tongue tacos, and because Jane liked tongue tacos, I invited her over.

And I don't know if it was the idea of tacos, or the plaintive tone in my voice, but she said she would stop by later. Alan lived in Santa Monica, so I had some time.

I went to several stores to get the various ingredients, boiled the tongue and took off the white coat of skin that covered the taste buds. I set the table with a linen tablecloth, fresh tortillas, Mexican beer, and I put out bowls of lime and cilantro and chopped tomatoes. I fried the tongue in one of Alan's frying pans, getting it good and salty and flavorful, and when Jane arrived we ate the tacos and drank the beer, and the tacos were excellent and the beer was good and everything was fine except for one thing.

No. That's wrong.

Everything was fine.

Love is all you need. That's what the Beatles sang,

and I wanted to believe it. I wanted to imagine love, to say *yes* to love, to tell Jane I loved her and mean it. And I might have been able to do all that except for one thing. Steve.

After we ate, we sat on a sofa underneath a window, lying back on the soft cushions, and I said, "Do you want to watch a movie?" Alan had a large collection of movies.

"We could watch a movie," she said. But she could tell, I think, that we weren't going to watch a movie.

We had developed a habit, and part of the habit included the habit of Steve. It was a habit linked in my mind—and hers too probably—with closeness and warmth and physical attraction, and it was a fine habit as far as it went, and because it was all we knew, we started doing it, together, going through the motions, pretending that what we used to have still existed. At a certain point she leaned back on the sofa, raised her hands over her head, and almost without thinking I rolled on top of her and we started kissing. When we started taking off our clothes it all seemed very natural. When she pulled down her tights and I took off my various shirts and she unbuttoned the buttons of her print dress, it all seemed normal enough, and normally when we put our mouths together she enjoyed it, and she would have enjoyed it now except the mouth that used to be there wasn't there. It wasn't Steve's mouth anymore, and that was the problem. We had drifted apart, not for lack of affection, but for lack of Steve. I wasn't being Steve, and maybe she realized it, or maybe she expected it. Whatever it was didn't matter, just like the conversation didn't matter, or how we sat on Alan's overstuffed blue sofa didn't matter, because what mattered happened on the bed.

We'd come to an unspoken agreement that we were going to make love on the bed. Or maybe it was a spoken agreement because I remember she didn't say "make love," she said "fuck," but still, I held the fleshy mounds at the base of her thumb and led her to the bedroom. I told her about a movie I'd seen in which a man blindfolds a woman, ties her to a bed, and makes love to her, and because we'd tried almost everything else, that's what we did. We took off the rest of our clothes and I found a pair of socks and tied her hands to the top of the black bedstead. She had long, thin legs and a tight strong belly, and she lay back on the bed while I tied the fairly loose knots. I wasn't especially turned on by the cotton socks holding her arms, but there we were. I found an airline sleep mask in a drawer by the bed and I used it to cover her eyes, and at first she didn't like it because she couldn't see, and she liked to see, but she didn't

resist. It was clear from her docility that this was going to be my experiment, as if, like a challenge, she
was saying, Show me something new. And because I
wanted something new, I knelt between her legs.
They were spread slightly and I spread them even
more. She was waiting there, quiet and passive, and all
the things I used to do, I did. But all those things
weren't having the desired effect. I put my tongue
where it liked to go, and moved my tongue, up and
down and sideways, above and below and all around.
I knew what she liked, or what she used to like, and
according to plan, this would be the moment when,
pretending to be Steve, I would get an erection, and
after some general preparatory touching we would
start fucking, as she liked to say. But in saying no to
Steve I was saying no to myself, and where Steve had
been, now there was a void. And nothing was filling
that void. I certainly wasn't, and as my tongue did its
thing, circling around the center of her sensitivity,
she wasn't getting excited, and I wasn't either. My
dick, or my mind, or more accurately my imagina-
tion, wasn't getting aroused. And without arousal,
well, I could kiss her where she liked to be kissed,
that's true, and I did. And at the same time I was
manually trying to stimulate myself. But none of it
was working. There was no question in my mind that
she was beautiful, or beautiful enough, so it wasn't

about her beauty. Or her willingness. Or the time of day or the color of the walls. It was my own unwillingness I was straining against. I could feel the sweat seeping out of my armpits and I could tell my unwillingness was winning. And I don't remember if I held her arms, or if I kissed her breasts or the skin at the base of her neck. I remember that after a while she easily slipped her hands out of the loose knots, pulled up the sleep mask covering her face, and she looked at me. We both knew what it meant. Nothing was said and nothing needed to be said. We rolled away from each other and lay on the bed.

In the movie *Detour*, the main character has taken on the identity of Charles Haskell, who died at the side of the road, and by becoming Haskell he acquires money and a car and the possibility of getting what he wants—the girl he loves. His plan is to find her, then abandon the role of Haskell, and become who he really is. And it would all be smooth sailing except the woman hitchhiker he picks up knows about Haskell. She knows about his pretending to be Haskell, and when she reads a newspaper story about a possible inheritance, she demands that he *keep* pretending. And for a while he does. For a while there's the hope that it's only temporary, that he's only temporarily staying with her and planning his life with her. He thinks it can't go on, but it does go on, and he hates it. The woman continues blackmailing him, and because he doesn't believe he can do anything, he plays along until, after one of their frequent arguments, she takes the phone into the bedroom. They're holed up in a rented room in downtown Los Angeles and she closes the door and he can hear her talking to someone and he would like to talk to someone, and at a certain point he can't stand it anymore. He gets tired of pretending. What seemed like a possible utopia has turned into the opposite of utopia, and because he wants the phone, he takes hold of the phone cord and begins pulling, pulling and pulling until finally it stops being pulled. Suddenly the room gets quiet. He opens the door, walks to the bed, and finds her body, limp and dead, lying on the bed, the phone cord, like a noose, wrapped around her neck.

I looked up. There was Jane, buttoning the buttons of her dress. She was standing and I was lying on the bed, and although I knew what she probably wanted, at that point I was tired of pretending. We both were. I was tired and she was tired, and we could both see that life wasn't long enough to keep pretending. In an effort, I suppose, to facilitate the end of that pretending, I sat up.

"At some point," I said, "we should talk."

"Let's do that."

And then we stopped talking.

She was dressed and I got partially dressed and we were standing next to each other, facing each other, looking into each other's eyes. We were very still. And the thing about stillness, it's infectious, and because we were still, we got more still.

She was very still when she said, "Goodbye."

I admired her honesty.

She slipped into her shoes, and I said something like "I'll see you" or "I'll call you," or actually I said, "I like you," which sounds odd, but I did, and then she turned and walked to the door.

I was expecting myself to say "Wait" or "Don't go," or something. But I didn't know what to say. So I didn't say anything. And she didn't say anything. And when she walked out the door the room became very quiet.

There was something about Charles Laughton. Although I looked nothing like him and my life was nothing like his, I found his inability to locate happiness intriguing. He used to say he "liked to imitate great men," meaning, I think, that he used the Hunchback of Notre Dame and the not-quite-human Caliban to show the world who he was. That made him happy, but because he didn't always know who he was, and because most of the time he hated who he was, performance was often frightening. He also said, "Before you amuse others, you have to amuse yourself," and during the dress rehearsal of *Galileo* I think he was trying to do that. An audience had been invited to this particular rehearsal, and the temperature in Los Angeles at the time was reaching the mid-nineties. Whether it was the heat or Laughton's idea of what Galileo would do, there he was, standing center stage, one foot propped nonchalantly on the other, one hand on his hip and one hand deeply inside his pocket—a pocket sewn onto his costume by Brecht's wife. He was playing pocket pool, scratching his balls and maybe more, and yes, he was revealing himself, but some people in the audience didn't want to see what he was showing. They wanted something else. He was showing them a part of themselves they were happy to overlook, and some of the people, somewhere in the darkened theater, began making noise. He'd created the façade of Galileo, but the façade was falling away. He was revealing his fear and his anger and his sexuality, and he was willing to do it and ready to do it except for the noise. The noise, to him, signaled distrust, and distrust, like a poison, was contaminating him.

And it wasn't just the audience.

A photographer friend of Brecht's—actually Brecht's mistress—had been taking photographs. She was up in the lights, on a gangway near the ceiling. Her camera was old and the shutter clicked when she took a picture. And it kept clicking, over and over. And it might not have been the clicking that bothered him, but something did, and he refused to continue. He was supposed to continue his act, but instead he exploded. At a certain point in the performance he just went berserk. He started screaming and yelling at the woman with the camera, looking into the lights and shouting up to her, and it looked as if he was shouting up to god. But it wasn't any god, and it wasn't really the person with the camera. It was him. He was stupid and fat and worthless, and he knew he was being an idiot but he couldn't help it.

The rehearsal was stopped.

Brecht, standing backstage, let him rant. He left him alone. *"Ich muss ein 7UP haben,"* Brecht said, and went out to the lobby for a soft drink. Joseph Losey, who had become the director after Orson Welles bowed out, found Laughton and tried to calm him down. They were standing in the wings. Laughton was shivering and Losey was holding him, by the shoulders. He was restraining him and at the same time trying to comfort him.

"Charles," he said. "You're just being a baby."

"Yes," Laughton said. "I am."

There's a famous line from the movie *The Wild Ones*. Marlon Brando, playing the part of a motorcycle rebel, has rolled into town, and when a townsperson asks him, "What're you rebelling against?" he says, "Whaddya got?" Although Brando was almost thirty when he made the movie, his character embodied adolescent rebellion, a protest against powerlessness, and against an adult world that constantly said he wasn't old enough or good enough. A child protests by saying no to authority because saying no is the only choice it has, and, like Marlon Brando, that's what I was doing, standing in a shower stall with Alan.

I'd picked him up that morning, at the airport, and he'd invited me then to what he called a "bathroom party" in North Hollywood. I wasn't busy that evening, so I went. I found the apartment, rang the bell, walked up the stairs and a few people were standing in the living room, but mainly people were in the bathroom, a large marble bathroom with a large Jacuzzi bathtub filled with cans of beer. There was also a shower stall near the door and chairs lined up against the wall, and some people were sitting on the edge of the tub. I didn't see Alan, but I heard his voice coming from the shower. "Come on in," he was saying, and I peeked over the top of the shower door and there he was, hair wet, drinking a beer with a group of people, all of them naked.

I took off my clothes in a room that, because it was being fumigated, was empty, and when I had everything off but my underwear, I stepped past the people sitting around the bathroom, and stepped inside the shower. It wasn't a big shower stall, but it was big enough. Alan welcomed me with a beer and introduced me to Amanda and Eliza and Vijay, and since everyone was naked, I slipped off my underwear and flung it into the hallway. When I asked them why they were wet, one of the girls turned on the water, which was cold at first and then warmed up, and we took turns under its spray, orbiting around in the stall, and although we were literally next to each other, we could move around without ever quite touching. I say "quite" because there was a certain amount of unavoidable butt bumping butt, and sometimes genital brushing against thigh. But it was all very relaxed and innocent, and somehow, being naked made everything seem funny. When someone accidentally opened the shower door, we thought that was funny. I was laughing and the girls were laughing and Alan took a bar of soap from the rack and started soaping up Amanda's back. She was short, and less voluptuous than Eliza, and she moved away her wet hair. Using the soap, Alan scrubbed her neck and her back and her side ribs, and when she lifted her arms he began soaping up her armpits and around to her chest, and then he handed the soap to me.

Vijay was smiling, and Eliza turned so that her back was facing me. Holding the sandalwood soap, I began massaging her tanned shoulders, rubbing suds across her back and upper arms, sliding it up and down her spine and down to her soft, slightly-less-tanned buttocks. I was reaching down, pressing my soapy arm against her wet skin, and she didn't seem to mind, and I certainly didn't mind, and I was surprised when Alan, at about that moment, told Eliza to look at me.

"Who does he look like?"

She cocked her head.

"I don't look like anyone," I said.

"Does he look like a movie star?"

"I'm not a movie star."

"I'm asking her."

"Which movie?" she said.

"Do your walk."

I'd told him about the Steve Martin walk.

"The one where you just stand there."

The problem was, I didn't want to do the walk.

"Come on," he said.

"Not now."

The girls were looking at me, and I was looking at Eliza's wet hair, and then Alan said, "Be yourself."

Normally those are very calming words. Normally they precipitate ease and relaxation, but under the circumstances, what were they supposed to mean? He had decided who I was and was trying to tell me who I was, and . . .

"Be myself?"

"Just do it."

"Do what?" I said. I was about to say, "Whaddya got?"

I wanted to tell him to fuck off, but the thing about anger, it needs an object, and Alan, the object I wanted to engage my anger with, wasn't playing along. He was standing there, squeezed between naked bodies, bemused and oblivious, and then he said, "You're acting like a child."

In *The Wild Ones*, the townspeople were scared of Marlon Brando, not because he was wild or seductive or tough, but because he was dissatisfied. He had an adolescent dissatisfaction, and the town fathers were afraid the dissatisfaction would spread. So they exercised authority. All rebellion springs from the unequal relationship of authority to non-authority—father/son, master/slave—whatever it is, the balance of power has to be unequal, and to Marlon Brando it was. He saw the inequality of power and he felt the need to protest, but because he was in a position of non-authority, he had to twist his protest, and transform his protest, and wiggle his protest into a place it could fit.

At a certain point Eliza pushed open the shower door and we all ran to the fumigated room. Someone grabbed a towel and we began drying each other, passing the towel between us, noticing as we did, the sizes of our penises and the different ways of trimming hair.

"Let's all go to my house," Alan said.

Alan wasn't a father figure, and as far as I knew he wasn't an authority on anything, but he wanted me to be something I didn't want to be, and the only response I knew was to protest. Protest has now become passé. We've seen so many struggles amount to so little that we've become numb, convinced of the ineffectuality of protest, but sometimes all we have is protest.

Vijay and the girls were drying each other, more or less ignoring Alan's invitation, and whether they would have been willing or not didn't matter because, when he suggested again we go to his house, I told him I wasn't interested.

"I don't think so," I said.

And it wasn't that I wasn't happy doing what I was doing. When I told him I wasn't interested, it had nothing to do with him or Eliza or my enjoyment of being in the shower, soaping up a naked body. I was like a kid saying, "I don't want to play," but really I did want to play. I did want to go to his house, but I was dissatisfied, and like a powerless child, the only thing I could do was *not* do. The only way I could protest was by saying no.

Saying no, however, can be a form of saying yes. That's what I was thinking. I was thinking about water, and like water cascading down a running brook, or like electrical impulses, or like anything really, we move along a certain path, and along the path there are forks going in different directions, and by saying no to one direction we automatically say yes to another. Like my brief career writing about movies. Since I didn't like the movies being made at the time, I wrote about other movies, older movies, movies that seemed better. I was saying no, and although I wasn't getting paid for it, by imagining something better, my saying no was a form of saying yes.

Earlier, when I'd picked Alan up at the airport, because I had time, I parked my car in the lot. I went into the actual airport building, and we all know what airports look like, and this one looked like that. Normally I would have found it sterile and loud and repulsive. But you can say no, not only to an event, but to a way of experiencing an event, and for some reason I said no to the way I normally looked at airports. And when I did, it didn't seem all that sterile. It was filled with human beings, living their lives and going about their businesses, and I felt oddly buoyed by the anonymity of watching them. The people were swirling around me, bored possibly, and preoccupied, and I was happy among them, and I walked for a while, through shops and seating arrangements, until I ended up in a small waiting area with an overhead monitor. I heard a voice recounting the news of a recent bombing. I watched an older couple walk through some yellow doors, and I'm going to skip how I ended up walking through the yellow doors myself, because the point I'm getting at happened when I got inside. First of all, it was quiet. It was a large room, bright, with leather sofas and chairs, cream-colored, and flowers on the table. People were drinking drinks and eating sandwiches, and quietly reading newspapers, which I noticed were mainly Italian. There were plenty of empty sofas so I sat on one, by a window, calmed by the luxury of the setting, or the modernity of the setting, or the air, which was very clean. The situation was foreign and I was foreign in the situation, and I watched people walking to their chairs from what I supposed was the bar, and my point about utopia is that we all know the condition of feeling satisfied or content, and then, after a while, we become dissatisfied or discontent. The requisites for happiness don't change, but we do, and I did, because suddenly I wasn't content to just sit there. I wanted to eat and drink, and the longer I sat there the more I wanted it. I watched a family in front of me, the kids polite, the father loving, the mother eating a sandwich, and although I knew the bar, in a place with well-dressed business-men and -women, would be expensive, I said no. I said it, not to what was around me, but to what was inside me, to the person (me) who considered an airport bar a waste of money. I wanted a sandwich, and when I went to the bar it turned out that there wasn't any bar. Behind an actual wooden wall was an area with a counter, and on the counter was a bottle of Prosecco sitting in a silver ice bucket. In a glass-front refrigerator there were elegant miniature sandwiches. I poured into an actual glass the sparkling wine, took from the refrigerator a sandwich on a plate, and I walked back to my comfortable sofa. And my point is that, yes, I'd lost my original utopia, but by saying no I'd found another.

It wasn't just happening with me. Jane was also saying no. I called her the following day, but she didn't answer. I called her a few hours later, and when she didn't answer I left a message, "Just checking in, hope you're all right," and when I called again and she still didn't seem to be answering, I decided to drive to her house. Which I did. I rang her bell and she came to the door, wearing pants and a man's white shirt, and let me in, but I could see that something was wrong. She smiled when she said hello, but instead of sitting with me or talking to me or looking into my eyes, she walked into her kitchen and began looking in her cupboards.

Water was boiling on her stove, and she was looking in her cupboards, at her tea selection, and she was having trouble choosing a tea.

"What are you looking for?" I said.

"Nothing," she said.

"Tea?"

"No." And then she turned off the stove.

When you like someone you want to make that person happy, and although the romance of our relationship may have been waning, I still liked her, and in an attempt to create a little happiness, I suggested we go out and find a tongue taco.

Tongue tacos were her favorite food, and the suggestion seemed to raise her spirits. Or maybe she just wanted to get out of her house. She closed the cupboard doors, and I drove her to a Mexican taco place near the corner of Sunset and Alvarado. We parked in the lot, got out of the car, read the hand-lettered sign advertising tacos *al pastor* and *pollo* and *carne asada*, but no *tacos de lengua*. A girl in a white dress said they would have tongue tomorrow.

I asked Jane if she wanted to try another place, but I could see that her thoughts had already moved on. She was looking at a sign hanging over an entrance about four doors down, to a pool hall. The sign was vintage and the windows were tinted, and inside it was large and dark, a cavern with pool tables and a billiard table, and there were two Ping-Pong tables in the back. We rented a ball and paddles from a muscular man, and I knew she'd played Ping-Pong before, but we'd never played together, and when we started playing I was surprised at how good she was.

We started hitting the little white globe back and forth across the net, and I didn't really spin it, and she was just hitting it, very mechanically. We were just warming up, and as we got warm, we began to get a rhythm, and as our volleys got longer, the activity of hitting the egg-sized ball became like a conversation, a sometimes exciting conversation. We didn't know when it would end or who would end it, and we didn't want it to end. The very idea of coordinating this perfect sphere to bounce between us was funny, and the way we tried to win without really caring who won, that was fun, and we probably could have kept the conversation going between us indefinitely, except for one thing.

We began to keep score.

Jane was balancing the ball on her paddle.

"You ready?" I said.

"Oh, I'm ready," she said, and we volleyed for serve.

She won the volley, and when the game began I could see she was serious about winning. She was slamming the ball and spinning the ball, and I was having a little trouble controlling the table, or more accurately, the ball on the table. I seemed to be hitting it off, or into the net, too busy returning her shots to land the shots I wanted to be making.

Then it was my turn to serve, and while she was taking off her sweater I could feel something happening to me. I should say that something was happening to Steve, because there I was, spine straight, holding the ball, and the feeling of Steve was fading. I should say I felt the desire to *be* Steve was fading. And as it faded I started winning points. The momentum shifted, and I became the one who was spinning the ball and she was the one having trouble. When she started serving, her serves, which had totally flummoxed me before, seemed like setups. And as I landed more and more of my trick shots, I could feel, not only confidence, but a kind of intoxication, and whether I was getting better or she was getting worse didn't matter. I was creaming her.

"You're sweating," she said.

And I was.

"It's not the Olympics, you know."

"No?"

And when one of my slams landed on the very edge of the table, I gave myself a point.

"That was off," she said.

"It was on," I said. "I heard it hit the edge."

"You couldn't've heard it."

"My ears are very sensitive."

"Are you saying it landed on the table?"

And right about then I realized that I wasn't making her happy. Steve, I knew, would want to make her happy, and yes, I wanted to make her happy too, but I also wanted to make myself happy. And being Steve wasn't doing it.

This is what I call the intoxicated-by-the-freedom-of-not-being stage. My whole relationship with Jane was based on me being Steve, and I'd proven that I could successfully do that, and now I no longer wanted to. I wanted, not just to win the game, but to control the game, and because we were keeping score, and because Jane was challenging my control, I couldn't stop. Or I didn't stop. I'd made an implicit agreement to play a role with her, and now I wasn't playing, and although Jane didn't acknowledge it, she could see what was happening.

In Brueghel's painting of Icarus, a plowman plows his field, a horse scratches its backside against a tree, and everything really does turn away quite leisurely from what is happening. Icarus, flying near the sun, had been warned by his father that his wings, made of wax, would melt. He was flying over a body of water, with fields and villages stretching out across the countryside, and Icarus must have been intoxicated by this sense of clarity and freedom. He was a young man, and he promised his father he would avoid the sun, but he couldn't seem to do that. I don't know if it was the heat or the light or the sense of freedom, but something drew him, and in Brueghel's painting we can see what happened when it did, a boy falling out of the sky.

And so I won the game.

And yes, I had a choice. I could have apologized, and offered to play another game. I could have tried to make that game different. I could have eased up and had a nice reciprocal Ping-Pong conversation. I could have said, I'll be Steve Martin, and volleyed with her in that back-and-forth way that, if it goes on long enough, creates a kind of habit in which the two individual players, because the ball is distracting them from who they are, forget who they are and merge into the other player, into one player really, one mind, playing an intimate and enjoyable game with itself.

But I didn't want to do that.

And since I didn't, and since she didn't want to play the game we were playing, I drove her home. We didn't speak the whole way back to her house. We didn't have to. We knew what goodbye felt like, and this was it, and after I dropped her off I went back to the Metropole. I bought a pack of peanuts from the vending machine by the door, then watched the crowd around the television set watching *Seven Brides for Seven Brothers*. I watched for a while and then I bought a second pack of peanuts, went up to my room, sat on my bed, my back against the wall, and ate my dinner.

Near the end of *Sunset Boulevard*, William Holden, playing the part of Joe Gillis, finally tells Gloria Swanson that he's leaving her. He's been working with the script girl on his screenplay project, which has become *their* screenplay project, and although they call the project *Untitled Love Story*, she's the fiancée of his best friend. So he says goodbye to her and drives up to the old mansion to finally tell Gloria Swanson the truth. She's waiting for him, and in my mind she's either dressed for a New Year's Eve ball, or else she's wearing a rejuvenating facial mask with only her eyes and her mouth left to communicate. I think Joe Gillis is wearing a tux, and anyway, they quarrel. That's a polite way of putting it because she's holding a gun, and she threatens to kill herself, and she's done this before so he knows, or thinks he knows, that the only way to deal with her and end their arrangement is to ignore her. And so he walks away. Which for her is unacceptable. She calls out, "Joe, Joe." She says, "I'll kill myself. I'll do it this time," but he walks away, out of the house, and when he gets near the swimming pool, that's when she fires the gun, and he falls, face-first, into the water.

 I had gone to a coffee shop in Venice, and I was sitting there with my paper cup of coffee, sipping through the hole in the lid, looking at the woman at the table in front of me. I was thinking about Joni Mitchell because this woman was wearing a beret. She had long blond hair, and I was looking at her and also looking out the window. I was thinking about how Venice was made to look like Mexico during the filming of the movie *Touch of Evil*. The street was lined with colonnades, made of adobe or adobe-like material, very Old World, or Third World, and as I sipped my coffee, looking out at the cars and the colonnades, I noticed the woman

walk out of the coffee shop. She had a posture not unlike Jane's, and I followed her. I walked, with my white paper cup, out to the street and down the street, following the hair of the woman who I knew wasn't Jane, but I followed her down toward the water. She sat on an empty cement bench along the curving path, and as I walked past her I turned my head to look out to the curving line of the horizon, not thinking about Jane or the woman or anything.

That's not completely true because, having said no to Jane and no to Steve and no even to myself, it didn't mean I wasn't having thoughts. Although I didn't feel like who I used to be, I must have been something. Unlike a Buddhist monk, some remnant of something was still inside my brain, the neurons still firing away, and I tried to control the firing by thinking, not about Jane, but about the waves on the shore and the sun on my neck. I walked up the path for a while, and when I turned around and walked back to the bench, the woman was gone. I didn't sit, but I stood there, looking at the bench she'd been sitting on. The back of the bench was covered with layers of advertisements, and I was mentally trying to strip away the layers, thinking that if I did this, I would eventually see what the bench really was. And if the bench was nothing but advertisement, then the bench wouldn't exist anymore.

That's what I was thinking when I heard a man running down the beach telling people to check something out. The man wasn't the Houdini I'd seen before. He was Houdini's P.R. person, and as he ran along the boardwalk, he stopped by the bench, pointed to the end of the jetty and said to me, "Check out the New Houdini."

"I've seen Houdini," I told him.

"Not this one," he said. "This is the New Houdini."

When I walked out to the end of the jetty, I wasn't surprised to see the same Houdini, in the same wetsuit, holding the same cinderblock, telling a crowd of teenagers to "check it out." He was asking for someone to verify the security of his bonds, and I turned to the person next to me. "I've seen this guy before," I said, and yes, he looked like the same man, but what if, beneath his skin, he'd changed? What if he wasn't who I thought he was? He was directing everyone's attention to the cinderblock and the chains around the cinderblock, and then he said to me directly, "Check it out."

Because of my new hairstyle I don't think he remembered me, or if he did, he made no acknowledgment. He stood by the railing with his cinderblock and his handcuffs, and no one else seemed to be moving so I said, "I think I've seen you before." But he wasn't listening. He was trying to build an audience. People were filling up the jetty and he was working the crowd, holding the cinderblock out to me, for me to inspect it, telling me, "Check it out, check it out."

The sky was overcast and the light seemed to be slowing things down, or else I was slowing down. I stared at the porous material of the cinderblock for a long time before I told him, "It looks fine."

"You sure?" he said. "Come on, don't let me off the hook," and he told me to test the weight of the cinderblock. But now, instead of the cinderblock, I was looking at the handcuffs. He had two handcuffs, one around each wrist, with a cable running between them.

"Why do you have *two* handcuffs?" I asked him.

"It doesn't make any difference."

"Why not just one?"

"It's all the same, man," he said. "It doesn't make any difference."

I was looking at the slightly gray stubble on his cheek, and beneath his cheek I could see his muscles tense. He'd probably jumped off this pier a hundred times, and he probably wanted to keep jumping, but when voices in the crowd began mumbling about the extra handcuff he acquiesced. He let the P.R. person take off the second pair of handcuffs, binding him with just the one.

And then, holding the cinderblock, he got up on the railing. His white, slightly pink toes were curled, as before, over the edge of the railing, and he stood there, as before, looking into the water and hyper-ventilating. He was waiting. We were all waiting, and as I watched him standing there, his legs trembling, proclaiming something about Houdini or the Great Houdini, I wanted to tell him that he didn't have to jump. "We all know you can do it," I wanted to say.

And that's when he jumped.

Holding his cinderblock anchor, attached by the one handcuff, he finally jumped into the water. It happened suddenly, and we all hurried to the railing, leaned over and looked down. The ripples were spreading out from the spot where he jumped. A few bubbles came up and we waited. Again, the water where he jumped was smooth. No kicking, just the unbroken water, and all of us waiting for the kicking. And at first I thought it would probably come, that if I waited long enough he would probably come back up. But the kicking never came.

All these people had gathered around, looking into the water, wanting him to come back up and hoping he would come back up, and I knew it wasn't going to happen.

I took a deep breath and held it as long as I could. There were still a few people standing on the pier when I walked away, mainly fishermen holding their

poles. I walked to the beach, listening, but not looking back. I wanted to look back but I only listened. I
knew that he was dead. I was sad that he was dead.
And I was also happy. He was dead.

I wasn't dead, but my time
at the Metropole was over.
I'd told myself that I was
only going to stay a month there, and now the month
was over, and although Earl, the night man, had said
I could stay as long as I wanted, I decided to check
out. The Metropole had become comfortable to me,
and however pleasant it was, I didn't want to keep
staying in a transient hotel. So I packed up my computer and my clothes and what few books I had, said
goodbye to Earl, and my plan was to drive out to the
desert, to camp in the desert for a while as a way to
sort things out. But Los Angeles was my desert.

So I drove around, looking for a hotel that would
be an upgrade from the Metropole. I started in the
downtown area, and when I didn't find anything
there, I enlarged my search, driving into various neigh-
borhoods. It had already gotten dark by the time I

drove up Chávez Avenue and found a motel that was called The Paradise. But it was too expensive. So I kept driving, and Chávez turned into Sunset, and I found another motel, which had no rooms, and then another, farther down Sunset, where an Asian man told me to come back the next day. I ended up spending the night sleeping, or trying to sleep, in the backseat of my car.

In the morning I got up, had coffee and a chocolate doughnut at a Chinese doughnut shop on Sunset and Fountain. And then I started driving again, not driving back to the Metropole, and in fact not driving anywhere, just randomly driving the streets of Los Angeles, driving without direction until, my bladder full and my gas tank low, I stopped at a taco stand. On the corner of Beverly and Normandie. There were mini-malls on three of the corners, but my corner was occupied by this taco stand, a brick structure, not the ideal taco stand with a lady standing by a fresh mound of cornmeal, but there I was, my hands on the polished cement counter. I bent down to talk into the small window, and it wasn't well lit back in there, but I could see a young man waiting to take my order. I asked him if he had a bathroom in his taco stand and he said that he didn't, but that the Korean restaurant across the street did. I could see his cheekbones in the dim light, and without a lot of effort I was able to see the skeleton he was beneath his skin and muscle, like a tar-pit animal in the middle of its dream.

I'd been trying to eat tongue tacos lately, partly because of Jane, but also because tongue, or *lengua* in Spanish, means language, and languages are founded on words, and it was a kind of invocation. Words can precipitate change, and even if cows themselves were incapable of using words, I thought in some undefined way that if I ate enough *tacos de lengua* the tongue might facilitate some . . . I didn't know. I ordered a tongue taco, paid the man, told him I'd be back, and went across the street to the Korean restaurant.

It wasn't a restaurant. It was a fast-food place with an ordering counter in front of the entrance doors. I looked up at the menu, as if I was thinking about making an order, and then quietly and quickly, I walked around the corner to where the bathrooms were, down a gauntlet of brightly lit tables, past people eating food, vaguely aware that lives were being lived in the moment of my passing.

I tried the door to the men's room but it was locked. I noticed the coin slot in the door. It was a pay-for-use bathroom, a quarter to pee, and I didn't have a quarter so I went back to the counter. I waited in line with an older man and a young couple, and oddly, no one had any change. When I got to the front of the line I asked a thin kid in a purple uniform if he had change for a dollar, meaning would he give me some change for the bathroom.

He said I had to order something.

"I can't just use the bathroom?"

"You have to order," he said.

People were behind me in line and he was standing by his computer, waiting for me to order some food. I looked up to the colorful photos on the menu and said, "You must have tea."

I ordered a tea, with milk, and when he brought my tea and the change from my twenty-dollar bill he was very efficient, like a robot. And that was fine except my change ended up being bills and about seven cents. Maybe a third penny was in there, but still not enough to get me into the bathroom.

"Could I have change?"

He told me I had to buy something.

"I *did* buy something."

He asked the couple behind me what they wanted.

"You're not done with me yet," I told him, but he was talking to them.

"Your order please," he said to the couple, and they moved forward in the line so that they were standing to my left.

"Excuse me," I said. "I'm still here." But he didn't notice, and they didn't seem to notice, and I looked at the older man, who I thought might offer some support, but he was looking at the illustrated menu.

The couple ordered their food and ordered their drinks, and I was about to say something else but I didn't see the point. It was obvious, to them and to me, that I was superfluous. By becoming Steve and then becoming *not*-Steve, I'd become a nonentity. So I stepped away from the counter, past the condiment area, and because of the architecture of the place, I found myself walking down the gauntlet of tables and sitting on a bench at one of them. I was sitting there, facing the men's room door, thinking I ought to just pee in a paper cup, when the door suddenly opened. A man with a reflective vest walked out, and before the door could shut, I walked in.

I would have hoped for a cleaner bathroom, but since it was free I couldn't complain. I urinated in the urinal and washed my hands in the sink, watching my hands sliding around each other in the soap and then the water, and then the automatic hand dryer. And it's strange because if there's a mirror around, it's hard not to look. And I did look. And what I saw, literally, was the glass of the mirror. Not the image *in* the mirror, but the mirror itself. I knew I was there, in my peripheral vision, but I wasn't focusing on my image,

I was focusing on the actual glass. Partly, it was an eye muscle exercise, a perceptual recoordination, and partly I preferred to see only the glass. If I saw myself then I would exist, and I preferred a world without me, and without all the lumbering disappointment I seemed to carry. And for a while I was able to do this. I could control my vision, for a while, but eventually my eye muscles got tired, or my brain got tired, and when they did I focused, naturally, not on the glass, but on the image *in* the glass.

I remember thinking that if this was a movie, I would look into the mirror, and with all the significance of mirrors, I would suddenly see what I was and accept myself. With swelling music on the soundtrack, or maybe the ambient sound of traffic, I would go out into the world a new man, a changed person, full of understanding and love, and yes, I did walk out of the bathroom, into the world, but I could only *wish* I was in a movie. I could only *wish* that an actual change had taken place, that I would look up and be something different. I could only wish that the man at the ordering counter would look up and smile at me. I could only wish that Jane would suddenly appear, and unable to read the menu, she would turn to me. "Where have you been?" she would say. Or I would say it.

 The book I'd been reading contained the script of *Galileo*, as well as an account of how Brecht and Laughton worked together, translating the text of the play. Because Laughton spoke almost no German, and Brecht very little English, their primary mode of communication was gesture. And because the language of gesture is largely unconscious, they could act out their father-son relationship without ever being aware of it. Because it was a satisfying relationship, trust was developed, and trust bred more trust, and that's how it started, the collaboration and friendship between the self-confident Brecht and the insecure Laughton.

Mostly they worked in Laughton's house, on the edge of a cliff in Pacific Palisades. It had a view and a garden, and Laughton, who was a large man, was an avid gardener. He would putter from the rosebushes to the lemons to the flowers in his terra-cotta pots. For him, a garden was a paradise, and Brecht seemed to understand that the puttering and the pacing and the piles of unread books were a part of a process that made the acting possible. Although Laughton was married, he was probably homosexual, and although

Brecht derided homosexuality, if love is to some extent the acceptance of an incomprehensible point of view, Brecht had a soft spot for Laughton's eccentricities. You can almost hear the acceptance in his journal entry: "Often L. would come and meet me in the garden, running barefoot in shirt and trousers over the damp grass . . ."

One afternoon, after a long period of heavy rain, they were sitting around Laughton's fireplace. The rain had stopped, and in the middle of reading some lines of the text, in the middle of a momentary silence, they heard a noise, a rumbling, like the earth moving, and they felt it move. When they stepped outside to check the hillside behind Laughton's house, they saw that part of the hillside had fallen away. The ground had seemingly opened up, and part of the cliff, and the garden that sat on the cliff, was gone.

I don't know what happened exactly, but I imagine Brecht standing by the patio doors, watching Laughton walk across the wet grass, his hands holding the sides of his head. If he went crazy over a misplaced prop, now, seeing his paradise ruined, what would he do? Brecht knew Laughton would be devastated, and of course he was, and in the face of that devastation he had a number of options. He could fall to the ground sobbing; he could look to the sky and berate the heavens; or, instead of lamenting the loss of what used to be or what might have been, he could walk out to the edge of what remained of his garden and kneel on the wet grass. Near the edge of the cliff some pots had fallen over, and I imagine him going to these pots, and the ones he could reach, he set them to rights. Brecht watched him as he kneeled on the grass, one hand on the grass and the other hand reaching out into the mud. Laughton's hands were his tools, and they were wet, and with them he reached out to the still-living roots. He scooped up what soil he could salvage, and he replanted the roots in the pots that were still unbroken. This was the situation that had presented itself, and he wasn't manic and he wasn't methodical. And it wasn't a role he was playing. His utopia had been destroyed, and this was his form of protest.

At that moment, Jane is visiting her friend Christine. Christine lives with her kids off Mulholland Drive, in a house with a redwood deck that overlooks the San Fernando Valley. Christine has been invited to a party, and because

Jane is feeling a numbness in her mind, and because that numbness is spreading to her body, and because she wants to feel something other than numbness, she agrees to go. She eats leftover birthday cake with Christine and Lucca and Isabel, and when the babysitter arrives, Jane drives with Christine, through the rain, down the winding road into Hollywood. Christine goes to a lot of clubs, and this particular club is meant to look like a Transylvanian castle, with stone blocks made of painted plywood. The music is loud and the crowd is vibrating, and everyone seems to glow with the glow of a tanning bed or a skin treatment, or the glow of sexual desire. The women, with their bronze skin, all seem to be perfect, their perfect breasts like pieces of jewelry attached to their chests. Although Jane is feeling removed from the bodies and the people inhabiting them, in their seeming happiness it's as if they've seen the light, or some light, some light Jane hasn't seen, and as she makes her way around the club she's aware that men want to talk to her. And it's nice to be noticed, to feel another person's desire directed at her, but her desire, which normally might respond to another person's desire, is somewhere else.

She joins Christine at a small table presided over by a Ghanaian diplomat. People come to the table because of the bottles of vodka, and Jane can't tell who's supposed to be pouring, but when she reaches over, someone fills her glass. She notices a tall body-guard standing in the corner watching the table. Then a man, who seems to have barely begun shaving, walks up to her and asks her if she wants to dance. She answers honestly, that she does, and when he invites her onto the dance floor she follows him. The music plays, and her body begins moving to the music, and although the man is watching her and smiling at her, instead of alleviating the numbness, his attention just seems to exacerbate it. And when the dance is over she thanks the man and walks back to the Ghanaian party. The bodyguard is still there, watchful and quiet, and although he's beneficent enough, as she sits under the sphere of his security, she wants to get away from that security. So she wanders to an outdoor alcove protected from the drizzle.

That's when another man approaches her, and like trying a different style of yogurt, or a different pair of shoes, she dances with this man. But she feels with him the same inability to dance. He wants to dance in a certain way, and get close to her in a certain way, and the only way she can get comfortable is to numb herself, to close her eyes, ignore his presence, and dance, not with him, but with herself. She can still dance, she thinks, but only with herself. And when the song ends she opens her eyes, and that man, like the other man, walks away. When she finds Christine, although Jane doesn't say anything, Christine can tell that the plan to jettison numbness didn't work. She can sense her friend's agitation, and although she's been happily flirting with a blond-haired man, she leaves that man, and they gather their things and they drive back home.

That night Jane sleeps on Christine's sofa. Because it's a strange place to sleep, she wakes up early. It's barely light. Everyone else is still sleeping, so she walks out onto the deck. She notices a bougainvillea, and although she knows the flowers have no scent, she bends a purple flower to her nose. Flowers are one of the things that used to give her pleasure, and she still has hope. Because the deck is perched above a canyon, when she looks out over the edge of the deck she holds the railing. From the promontory of the deck she can see, as the sky begins to lighten, the lingering lights of the city below her, fading away. She feels the air in her lungs, and she's listening to the air, and the birds in the air, and the sound of traffic in the distance.

When the family wakes up, they all sit around a big table and eat pancakes together. Later, while Christine is going over some math homework with Lucca, Jane walks out to the deck and stands on the deck, looking at the view. It was raining before but now it isn't, and Isabel, who is seven years old, is also standing on the deck, in front of a redwood picnic table, wanting to cry and trying not to. Yesterday she had a birthday party, and one of the gifts she was given by her father, Christine's ex-husband, was a socket set, a perfectly good set of tools for doing specific work. And you might think that tools are wasted on a young girl, that they're only valuable for the work they perform. But Isabel loved the tools, not for their intended purpose, but as beautiful objects. The problem is, she's left the tool set out in the rain and now the tools are wet. She's staring into the plastic container filled with the different-sized sockets, looking at the ruined tools but not touching them. Jane walks to her. She sees the tears that Isabel is trying to contain and she recognizes those tears. She tells Isabel that water isn't necessarily a problem, that the tools can probably be salvaged, but to the young girl they're already ruined. What used to be pristine and beautiful has now been destroyed, and no amount of wishing is going to save them. And that's probably true, Jane thinks, but she also thinks it might not be true. She brings the tool set into the house, sets the red container on the kitchen table, finds some rags, and first alone, and then with Isabel, begins working. Together they take out each individual socket, dry each one,

198

and then they dry the plastic container. It doesn't seem extraordinary to Jane, not at first. They're just working together. But as Jane stands with the girl, not speaking, cleaning and drying and polishing the stainless pieces of metal, she can feel a sense of possibility rise up in her and come to the surface. And once it's there, she doesn't want it to go away.

Los Angeles has been called the City of Dreams; also the City of Angels; Jim Morrison called it the City of Lights, but to me it was just a city. I said in the beginning of this book that I'm originally from New York, but that's not true. Although I did live in New York for a number of years, I was born in California, near San Diego, and for that reason Los Angeles has never been a dream for me, just a city, a city to live in. Nathanael West called it the City of Death, and maybe it was for him, but for me, at the moment, it was something else. At the moment I was walking along Vermont Avenue, alive in a way I'd never been before, alive to my senses and the world streaming in through my senses. I'd detached who I was from the web that had organized my world, and although a sense of self is a wonderful thing, as I walked along the sidewalk that morning, listening to the sounds of the cars, and the birds, and the occasional voices, I didn't need any mediation between me and the world.

I'd parked my car in the post office parking lot, so it must have been a weekend day. Not that weekends meant anything to me. Not that anything meant what it normally meant. I was walking along the street, the sun in the sky, and I passed a bank where people were getting money. I didn't get money. A white butterfly, or possibly a moth, flitted in front of me. The bookstore I liked was across the street, but the idea of reading symbols on pieces of paper seemed ridiculous. I was walking past a tree, and if I wanted to read something I could read the tree. Not read, but see, in the tree, whatever I wanted to know about the world. The tree was alive and the plants planted in front of the bank, they were alive, and under the sidewalk a root of the tree was pressing up, lifting the sidewalk, and I placed my foot on the section of cement, balancing first on that foot, and then the other, walking along like that until I came to a corner.

Across the street to my left was another corner, and I aimed my mind in the direction of that corner. I stepped off the curb, placing one foot on the black asphalt of the street. I heard the sharp wail of a car horn and then, a half second later, a car passed in front of me, inches from my chest. The car and the horn drove away and a woman with a baby stroller said something to me. She looked worried. "I'm fine," I remember telling her. She probably thought I was crazy, stepping in front of a moving car. *"Dónde vas?"* she said, and why did she want to know who I was? *"Dónde vas?"* she said again, and then she pointed to the stoplight. *"Esta seguro,"* she said, smiling now, indicating that now I could walk. And I saw no cars coming, so I stepped off the sidewalk, telling myself I was fine. I crossed the street, and I could see people sitting outside, in the sunshine, in front of a Starbucks store. It was a coffee store, with tables, and that's what I wanted, I thought to myself, not a coffee, but a place to sit. Not in the sun, so I walked inside the glass doors. It was cool, and warm, and there were people. I was amazed by the people, so intent on their work or their conversations. There weren't any vacant chairs so I sat on the floor, legs crossed, my back against the wall. I assumed people were watching me, but that's what I like about a city. Nothing is strange in a city. A man and a woman were sitting at a nearby table. The man was eating a cookie, and although there was music in the room, it was background music. Noise. And it mingled with the music of the noise of everything else. A man to my left was looking at his computer. A potted plant with long green leaves was to my right. Then the woman at the table stood up, the man ate the last of his cookie, and the woman positioned a bag on her shoulder. When they left I went to their table. No one seemed to notice that I wasn't eating or drinking or using the products being sold. From the table I could see the whole room and the light of the room, coming from the street and the overhead bulbs and the people. I noticed the light given off by people, by their bodies. It wasn't a blinding light, but I could see it, see them, and it was something I usually didn't see. I'd never noticed so much light before, and music. The air conditioner seemed to be playing music, but no one was moving to the music, and I suspected that only I was hearing it. And seeing the light. And the raisin. A folded, slightly scrunched-up piece of tissue paper was still on the tabletop, and on the paper there were crumbs from the cookie, the oatmeal cookie, and along with the crumbs was a raisin. The raisin had been baked, so it was doubly shriveled, and I thought maybe I'd feel sorry for the raisin, shriveled up, left behind, unwanted, but the raisin wasn't sad. It wanted nothing. Or maybe it wanted to be eaten. I hadn't eaten for a while, and not having eaten, I could feel my empty stomach. And although I liked it empty, I picked up the raisin. And when I say light was emanating from the raisin, I don't mean actual light. It was more like glowing. The raisin was glowing with its raisinness. And when I say the raisin was talking to me, I don't mean actual speech. But by virtue of its raisinness and its luminosity, I got the idea that I should eat the raisin. I was holding it between my fingers, and there was the music of the world swirling around me, and the light bouncing off the objects around me, and also bouncing off me, back onto the objects of the world. I looked at the raisin, large and dark, with a sugar crystal clinging to its skin. The raisin contained an entire world, and I put that world to my lips, opened my lips, and let the raisin fall onto my tongue. I held the raisin in my mouth, feeling my saliva surrounding the little black seed, and then, with my front teeth, I bit the raisin in two. I could taste some sweetness when I did, and I let that sweetness slide over my tongue, and the idea of my tongue reminded me of Jane. I imagined her cheeks when she smiled, and then I bit the two halves of the raisin so that now there were four halves, or four parts, and I let my saliva and the raisin—it wasn't a raisin anymore—mix in my mouth, and then I positioned the raisin back on my teeth and I began chewing. And the thing that had once been a raisin sent sweetness into my mouth, and when I swallowed I could feel the sweetness of what was no longer a raisin, but was now something else, something transformed, and I could feel it seeping its way down my body and into my body, and I could feel it, in my arms and legs and brain even, the nourishment of it, the sweetness and life, and *Man ist was man isst,* I thought, and like an elixir coursing through my arteries, it was flowing through me, altering my blood and the cells that were fed by that blood, and I don't know how long I sat at the table, but at some point I looked up and I realized that yes, the world was still there.

Jane was standing on the deck—taking in the view of the San Fernando Valley—when her phone rang.

"Hello?"

"It's me," I said. She didn't recognize me at first because I was using Scott's phone.

"Where are you?"

I was sitting in my car on some street. "Where are *you?*"

"Watching a movie," she said.

She explained that she was at Christine's house, watching Isabel following her brother around the house, filming him with a camera. When I asked if I could drive up and visit her there, she told me later, that later would be better, and we agreed to meet at the café we'd been to on Sunset.

I found a place to park in the same neighborhood I parked the last time I was there, and when I walked into the restaurant Jane was already sitting at a table. She had her back to the window, and I sat across from her, facing the window.

She was wearing a sleeveless dress, and I felt like raising my water glass and making a toast, to the dress or to her, and I was thinking about what exactly I wanted to toast when she said, "Not with water." Apparently you weren't supposed to make a toast with water, but since my glass was raised, she raised hers. It had a piece of lemon floating in with the ice, as did mine, and we touched the rims of our glasses. I'd heard somewhere that when you raise a glass it's considered polite to look at the person, so I looked at her, and for a moment she looked at me, and then we drank.

I ordered a chai with milk, Jane ordered an omelet with fries, and I noticed that, when she ordered, the table rocked slightly. When I jiggled it, I could see which leg was causing the wobble, so I grabbed a paper napkin from under my knife, folded the napkin, and bent down. I was kneeling under the table, my head under the table, lifting the uneven table leg and placing the folded napkin under the leg, when I saw her face poke down. She was looking at me.

"Better?" I said.

"Better," she said.

And that's when our food came. We sat there, eating and talking, like something we'd done a thousand times, but now it seemed . . .

"How was your day?" I said.

"What I did?"

"Or later."

"Do I have plans, you mean?"

She moved a small vase of flowers to the side of the table and then slid the plate of french fries to a point equidistant between us. We ate french fries together, and when they were gone, all I could think to say was "You look different," because she did.

"Than what?"

"What I imagined."

"Thank you," she said. "I guess."

Then we paid the bill. She drank the last of the water from her glass, placed it on the round water mark, exactly where it had been before, and when she looked up, I saw her eyes and the life that seemed to spill out of them onto her face.

"Shall we go?" she said.

She stood up and then I stood up, and she announced that her car was around the corner.

In the Hitchcock movie *North by Northwest*, Cary Grant plays a man who's mistaken for a spy. At first unwittingly, then grudgingly, and then, when he meets Eva Marie Saint, with a kind of relish, he actually becomes a spy. Near the end of the movie Cary Grant and Eva Marie Saint are chased to the cliff above Mount Rushmore. Below them are the faces of the presidents, staring out over the visitor center, and beyond that, to the Great Plains. Martin Landau, part of a gang of actual spies, is trying to kill them. He's chased them to the edge of this cliff where they slip somehow and fall off the cliff, and they're hanging on to the stone face of whatever president it is. We can see Cary Grant's fingers holding on, and we can see Martin Landau step up to the edge of the cliff and place his foot on Cary Grant's fingers. We can almost hear the bones in his hand crack, and he might easily fall to his death, but Cary Grant keeps holding on, and there's a struggle and at the end of the struggle Martin Landau is the one we see falling downward into space, getting smaller and smaller, until eventually he disappears.

I followed Jane, past the café tables and out into the sunlight, into the dry air and the evaporating clouds. We walked together around the corner and up the residential sidewalk, walking between the lawns, underneath the palm trees. When she saw her car she stepped into the street and was walking in the street and I was on the sidewalk. She walked to her car with her keys in her hand, and then, electronically, she unlocked the car doors. With a gesture of invitation she said, "Are you coming?"

In her gesture there was ease and grace, and although the gesture itself could have meant any number of things, the beauty of the gesture was its tone. *Her* tone. They talk about dreams having a tone, and although I wasn't dreaming, I thought I understood what her tone was.

Theoretically I would have stepped off the sidewalk, onto the soft grass, and walked to the passenger door of her car. Theoretically I would have learned, from what I didn't do before, how I would now move toward happiness. I would walk to her passenger door and I would open it. It would have been very easy. But instead of doing that, I stepped over the grass and off the curb, and I walked to the street to where she was standing.

"You're not coming?"

I was standing on the asphalt, looking at Jane and the palm trees lining the street behind her. I was inside my body, in with all the millions of habits I'd spent my life creating. Her invitation was an invitation to be in the world and to see the world in a new way, to see her in a new, and therefore unknown, way. Going to my car and driving off alone, that was already known, and I felt the lure of the already known. She opened her door and stood by her door, holding the door with her hand. I was about to tell her about my car, that I was parked in a different residential neighborhood, in a one-hour-only zone, and I could feel myself about to speak, but as I was about to speak, instead of speaking, I remembered something. I remembered Cary Grant in *North by Northwest* reaching across the brow of one of the presidents, taking the hand of Eva Marie Saint, pulling her off the face of the president and into his arms.

I'm standing in the street, the image of Cary Grant in my mind turning into an image of Steve Martin, then turning into a single thought: If I'm going to become something, why not become something with Jane. She's looking at me and I'm looking at her, and the distance between us is like an ocean. And I'm thinking about the ocean, and about how water, when it flows down a stream and enters the ocean, is doing the necessary thing. I know I'm breathing because I can feel the breath coming into my lungs and then leaving my lungs and oddly, it's happening on its own. I see Jane, wedged between the door and the car, and it's as if I can see myself. I see myself turn to my right and take a step. I take one step, then another, watching myself as I walk away from the place where I'm standing and the skin I'm standing in. I watch myself walk away from myself, around the back of the car, onto the grass and across the grass to the passenger door. Part of me is standing on the asphalt, watching, and part of me walks to the door. It's unlocked, so I open it. We both get into the car at the same time, and then she closes her door. I look over at her, fitting into the cushion of the seat, her hands in her lap, the steering wheel in front of her. The keys are in the ignition. She's looking through the car window, and the light is diffuse but sharp. We're both aware that I'm looking at her, and then she turns to me and looks at me. I see, as if through my eyes, and I see her entire face. I see the contours of her cheek and the shine on her nose and the freckles below her eyes. I can see her eyes looking into my eyes. She's looking into my eyes but she's seeing the person behind those eyes.

"Okay?" she says.

"Okay?"

"Are you ready?"

And I'm not ready. I'll never be ready. "I'm ready," I say, and I close my door.

She starts the car.

She turns the wheel, pulls out of the parking

spot, and as we drive up the tree-lined street I turn around. Looking back through the window of the car I can see myself, still standing on the asphalt, a hand raised as if waving. I can see the palm trees receding, and I see myself, a human figure, standing there, watching me getting farther and farther and farther away, until eventually I disappear.